Comfort Food

Comfort Food

Kitty Thomas

Burlesque Press

Comfort Food

Printed in the United States of America

ISBN-13 978-0-9819436-6-4
ISBN-10 0-9819436-6-7

Wholesale orders can be placed through Ingram.

Published by Burlesque Press

Contact: burlesquepress@gmail.com

To Silence.
Not always the enemy of communication.

Acknowledgments

Thank you to the people who supported and helped bring Comfort Food into existence.

K: for offering critique, feedback, copyedits, and for taking fifteen pictures of chicken noodle soup, which didn't end up making it into the final cover design.

M, C, and SEP: for beta reading.

C and J for their formatting help.

Disclaimer

This is not a story about consensual BDSM. This is a story about "actual" slavery. If reading an erotic story without safewords makes you uncomfortable, this is not the book for you. This is a work of fiction, and the author does not endorse or condone any behavior done to another human being without their consent.

ONE

The first day of my captivity was like being born . . . or dying. They're both kind of the same thing with the long tunnel and the bright light at the end. Maybe it wasn't like either, actually. Maybe I'm remembering it wrong because for me that day all there was, was darkness.

I was blindfolded, sitting in a hard metal chair, with each of my legs bound to a chair leg and my arms tied up behind me. The sharpest bit of sensory input I had was the silence. It was a suffocating blanket from which there was no escape. Unless I started talking just to hear my own voice, a desperation I refused to display in the first five minutes of consciousness.

I remember thinking this was how spy movies often started, with sensory deprivation: the first step to get the prisoner to spill his secrets. I had no secrets. I was an open book, and maybe that was the problem. I was a minor celebrity on the public-speaking circuit, self-assured, articulate. The poster-girl for everything others wished they could become. Not a threat to anyone really.

I'd written a few books and had started to grow a following of loyal devotees. Someone would notice I was missing, at least by the time my next speaking engagement rolled around in a couple of weeks.

The day had started at one such engagement. A very nice luncheon, in a very nice restaurant in downtown Atlanta had been booked for the event. I usually started and ended my book tours in Atlanta because it was close to my home in the suburbs.

The audience was mostly comprised of women, my primary demographic, though I'd never set out to become some *voice of women*. There was a smattering of men, but I wasn't paying much attention.

Women go through their lives a bit differently than men. We're always cautious. It's not that we live in abject terror twenty-four hours a day thinking some random man is going to come along and rape or kill us. Only the most neurotic of us think that way.

Still, you never know what kind of wacko out there has become fixated on you. And despite all the empowering speeches and the women's movement, in the grand scheme . . . women are prey.

This was the place I was at, the almost complete denial it had happened to me. Me, who is always so careful. Locks her doors, doesn't walk or jog with ear buds in her ears, doesn't take candy from strangers in vans. You know the drill.

I was listening to the silence and wondering how the hell this could be happening. Other things were running through my mind as well. Things that had me hoping maybe I *did* have some government secret and once I shared it, I could go on my merry way.

Rape. Death. Dismemberment. Maybe in that order, maybe not. Though that order would be preferable to Dismemberment. Rape. Death. Or Rape. Dismemberment. Death. You always want your dismemberment to happen after the death.

Death first would be the absolute best-case scenario. I'd seen enough woman-in-peril movies, and I was no

MacGyver. I didn't really have any kind of ballpoint pens on me that I could somehow get out of a pocket and turn into a ballistic missile.

My mistake was a stupid one. I'd left my drink unattended. Men never have to worry about this shit. I guess because statistically speaking there are fewer female psychos stalking men than the opposite, and most confrontations between men are pretty straightforward.

Like all women raised in the current climate of fear and loathing of men, I was taught never to leave my drink unattended. All women know this. We do. Even if we aren't explicitly told, it seems to come with the packaging and wiring of being female. Just common sense in the age of the date rape drug. Expecting even the most sensitive male to truly understand any of this is like expecting a wolf to understand the finer points of being a rabbit.

Still. We seem to think there are exceptions. Like my luncheon.

There are no exceptions. If there were, I wouldn't be sitting tied to a chair listening to the questionably comforting sound of my breath going in and out.

I couldn't stop thinking about how my parents were going to react to all this. My sister, Katie, had died several years ago in an accident. She was deaf and hadn't heard the car barreling around the curve. The driver wasn't used to ice on the road. No one in the south is. My parents hadn't spoken about her in years because they couldn't deal with it. I couldn't imagine how they'd cope with my disappearance and wondered if they'd curse God for doing this shit to them twice in a row.

The door creaked open then, exactly like doors do in scary movies. At least now I knew what kind of story I was in, no sense fooling myself about it. The sound of his boots echoed eerily loud on the concrete floor as he approached me. He stopped maybe a couple of feet away as the silence stretched on for a small eternity. Finally, I felt compelled to speak.

"Why are you doing this?" My voice shook when I said it, and I hated that. I sounded weak. I'd never sounded weak before in my life.

It was such a cliché question. If these were to be my last words, they felt like stupid and unimportant ones, but I had to know. Why *had* he taken me? Did I send out a vibe or was he just obsessed? Was there something about me that screamed *Victim*?

I'd always tried to give the impression that I wasn't easy prey. I'd been fooling myself. It had been ridiculously easy for him to take me.

Then again, maybe I was being all wrong-headed in assuming right from the start my captor was male. Theoretically, it could just as easily have been a woman.

Somebody jealous of my professional success. Someone who hated me for some imaginary reason, like that her husband thought I was pretty or something. As if I can control who thinks I'm pretty. There was always that one-in-a-million reason for some woman to go apeshit psycho on you.

And I don't hate men. There is a very small percentage of men who choose to perpetrate violence against women, despite the ease with which they can do it. Most women don't hate men. Those that do, though, probably do so not because most men are violent towards women, but that they could be, if they wanted to. This knowledge sets up a kind of helpless rage in some women. One I'd never succumbed to until today.

He still hadn't spoken. I was carrying on this internal monologue in my head because I was afraid I might say something that would get me killed. Or worse.

It was naive, but I wanted to believe I could somehow alter the course of events here by saying the right thing. My words, the thing that had made me so compelling to people, were more useless than I wanted to admit. My only weapon had the efficacy of a squirt gun.

I could feel the heavy lump forming in my throat as he stepped closer. I couldn't see him because of the blindfold still covering my eyes, but I knew he was observing me, probably taking me in with amusement. It pissed me off that he held my life in his hands, and yet he might be *amused* with me.

I continued to wait for him to answer the *why are you doing this* question, but the answer didn't come.

There is a standard victim/victimizer protocol, an etiquette if you will. *Why are you doing this?* is the introductory question, sometimes followed by screaming or crying. I wasn't screaming or crying. I wanted to conserve my energy for my one possible moment of escape. Eventually he'd do something stupid. He had to.

After the victim's opening line, the victimizer usually says something so terrifying the victim wishes they'd never opened their mouth. This man, however, seemed to be capitalizing on the terror of uncertainty.

After all, if he spoke to me perhaps there was something human in there, something I could reason with, some tiny, frail hope I could bargain somehow. A large, cool hand rested softly against my cheek.

There was no violence or threat in the way he touched me. It was my cheek, so it certainly wasn't an overly sexual touch. Still, it was a threat to me. It said, *I have no problems breaching your personal bubble or touching you at any time.*

His hand remained pressed solidly against the side of my face like that for a couple of minutes at least as my heart continued to hammer in my chest. That huge, strong hand. He could easily beat me to death with it, or he could be gentle. Although at this point, even gentle was an act of violence. I didn't know which I preferred.

With violence I could have the appropriate socially-approved victim response. I knew from experience anything else could produce a very different physical reaction.

At seventeen I'd gotten involved with my first real boyfriend. He was cute and had that edge of danger that girls of that age are so fond of. He gave off an air of something wild and frightening, and I'd been along for the ride

We'd fooled around a lot. My strict religious upbringing didn't allow for more without fear of God's wrath coming down on me, and orgasms weren't worth an eternity in hell. Though in hindsight, the idea that some deity could be bothered to punish any one individual for what they chose to do with their clothes off, seems stupid at best.

He'd pressed me down on the bed, my legs hanging over the edge. We were in his room; his parents were downstairs. The sounds of the nightly news drifted up to the bedroom. I was lying there, my pants forgotten on the floor, though I was still wearing a shirt.

He wanted to go down on me. It was more than I was ready for at the time, and I was paranoid about getting an STD, *the* STD. Yes, this was how empty my education in sexually transmitted diseases had been in the abstinence climate. Still, I'd said no. I'd meant no.

He'd ignored me, spreading my legs wide for his perusal, gripping my wrists tightly against my thighs as he held me down. "You'll like this, I promise," he said.

I struggled, but he was too strong, and I didn't have the proper leverage to shove him away. He buried his head between my legs, slowly laving the bundle of nerves there. I wanted to cry out, but I couldn't face the shame of his parents running up there and finding me half naked on his bed.

Somehow it was worse knowing I could have stopped him. It was one violation or another. His tongue on my clit, or his parents knowing what we'd been up to, thinking I was a slut.

"Please, please don't." I'd begged him, and yet he hadn't stopped.

It was incredible how little time it took for my resolve to melt, for "Please, no" to turn into "Oh God, don't stop."

When he was finished, I just laid there, my legs shaking from the force of my orgasm. They'd turned to jelly, and I felt weak, drugged in the post-orgasmic afterglow euphoria. The orgasm I couldn't possibly go to hell for. He looked up into my eyes, a self-satisfied smirk on his face and said teasingly, "I told you you'd like it. Now, what do you say?"

"Thank you." It was our little inside joke. It had never previously been applied to anything sexual. The words had slipped out of my mouth before I could stop them, and on some level they were true.

He and I never talked about the incident after that, and he never directly forced me again. He never had to. I didn't give him the opportunity because it was too confusing. In his mind, I'm sure he believed he hadn't done anything wrong, since he'd successfully changed my mind by turning my body against me. In the end I'd liked it. The entire sordid event from start to finish.

The juxtaposition of fear and helplessness, set up next to complete pleasure and eventual surrender. I'd masturbated for months afterward to the memory of the event. It was several years before I mentioned it to a friend.

She'd insisted it was no different than rape. I suppose she was right, but I'd never seen it that way. I'd for some reason never had the normal emotional response. I'd gotten off on it. Something was different in the way I was wired and that, perhaps, was the only thing that had saved me. Over time I developed an intense shame about it, not because I'd been violated, but because I wasn't properly traumatized by what had been done to me. Because I sometimes still touched myself thinking about it.

I thought he'd left me alone again, but then I heard another metal chair scrape against the floor. His heavy weight fell into it, and he placed something on a table. My breath hitched.

Moments later, a spoon was prodding at my lips. I opened my mouth, and warm chicken noodle soup slid down my throat. Comfort food. Oh, sweet irony. I wasn't worried he'd drug me. Why would he?

Drugging had been a convenience of transport. He had me where he wanted me, no doubt in some eerie sound-proofed basement cell. I heard him crumble crackers into the soup before feeding me another bite. I hadn't realized how hungry I was. Intense fear tends to shut down the hunger response.

After the second bite, his hand gently fondled one of my breasts through my clothing. I stiffened and flinched away. He didn't yell or hit me. He simply placed the bowl back on the table and got up. Then his footsteps started to recede in the direction they'd come from.

So this was the game he was playing? Either I would accept his touch, or he'd starve me to death? I hear it's a horrible way to die, second only to drowning or suffocation. Those things could still be on the menu. It was early yet.

"Please . . . wait." I hated myself for saying it. Hated myself enough that had my hands been free and a razor been nearby, I might have pressed the blade into my skin and bled out right there in front of him.

I was already bargaining, doing the *appease the captor and maybe he won't hurt you too bad* thing. In turn, he would show a small kindness here or there to gain my total dependence on him And voila . . . instant Stockholm Syndrome.

His footsteps stopped, and I heard him turn, still as silent as ever. After a moment, he returned and sat back down in the chair.

I was trying not to hyperventilate. I wasn't sure what I'd have to allow him to do to let me breathe into a paper bag. This was how our agreement began. He never said a word, never made any kind of verbal threat. He didn't need to.

It was a tacit agreement. I would give him what he wanted, or else. Right now the bargaining chip on the table was food. I was still arguing with myself over that one, berating myself for not being stronger, not holding out longer. He hadn't tried to fuck me yet. Having my breast fondled was a small price to pay to eat.

The spoon prodded at my mouth again and I opened up for the warm liquid. He'd gotten the good crackers. The oval-shaped Townhouse kind. The kind I liked. I had a moment of almost hysteria wondering how long he'd watched me, how much he knew about me. Did he know this particular food somehow idiotically made me feel safe?

I tensed as I heard the spoon clank into the bowl again. I knew what that meant. Every cell in my body felt poised, on edge, trying to inch away as his hand closed over my breast once again. He hadn't moved to take any of my clothes off. He seemed to want me to agree to every step of my desecration.

I didn't want to respond, but his thumb caressed over my nipple through the layers of clothing so gently, so enticingly that I found myself arching toward him. I wanted to jerk away, but if I did he'd leave and take the food with him. This time my begging might not bring him back.

This pattern repeated itself over and over. First a bite, then a fondle, until the soup was gone. He wanted to make sure the conditions were clear to me, that nothing would be given to me freely. I would pay for it all.

I kept rewinding the day in my head. What if I'd done something differently? What if I'd never left the table? Had it been necessary to reapply my lipstick that close to the end of the day? Had a tube of waxy color called *Sassy Vixen* really been the catalyst to take my freedom from me?

I knew it was crazy to think that way. He would have gotten me sooner or later if he was determined enough. That moment in time wasn't the definitive moment. I would have had another unguarded moment later and would have paid for it then.

We'd gotten through the bowl of soup and an awkwardness descended. It was as if he'd only planned this far and had no idea what his next step should be. Maybe he was waiting for me.

Okay.

"Please tell me why you're doing this." My voice was stronger now. Maybe it was the captive/captor alliance we seemed to have formed. He didn't seem the kind to lash out with no planning. He instead seemed the type who could wait multiple eternities for everything to work to his desire.

No reply.

He placed his fingers on my lips, gently silencing me. He had no intention of answering the question, and I had no power to make him do so. He knelt on the ground beside me and I heard the knife as it cut through the ropes binding my legs to the chair.

I had the urge to kick him in the face, but I didn't. If I kicked him, I was escalating the situation to real physical violence, and he would no doubt retaliate. This wasn't someone with gentlemanly scruples. Before I could make a solid decision against kicking him, my chance slipped away, as he moved behind me.

He sliced through the ropes around my wrists. I hadn't realized how much they'd cut into me, but they burned now that the air hit them. He came back to stand in front of me, bringing my arms around with him, placing my hands primly on my lap like I was a posable doll. I could barely feel myself breathing.

I have a deep and abiding fear of knives. Honestly, I don't know many people not afraid of knives. For most, a knife is scarier even than a gun. If someone kills you with a gun, it can be quick, painless. Knives don't offer that possible luxury. They are intimate and violent in a way a gun could never hope to be.

Despite my hands and legs being free, I still didn't fight back. He had a knife, and I was blindfolded. It didn't take a mathematician to work out those odds. Before I could reach up to remove the blindfold, his hands were encircling my wrists, rubbing them, as if he were actually concerned he'd hurt me.

But I knew that wasn't the case. Anyone who drugs you, kidnaps you, and locks you in a cell doesn't care if they hurt you. Maybe he just didn't want to hurt me, *yet.* In one quick movement, he ripped the blindfold away.

Although the scrap of dark fabric hadn't been pleasant, it had acted as a sort of safety, a filter. Now there was nothing between us. I looked into the coldest, blackest eyes I'd ever seen, fathomless pools of something I couldn't quite recognize as human. There was an otherness about him, something that made him different from me, from anyone I'd ever spoken to before.

I expected him to start the verbal threats now that the mystery of my captor was over, but he didn't. He just stared. I was his science project.

In another situation I would have found him attractive. He was muscular, had a firm jaw, great hair, not an ounce of body fat. I imagined this was what Ted Bundy's victims felt at some point, that it was utterly impossible he could want to hurt them and be so beautiful at the same time. The unbelievable shock someone so attractive could be a predator.

Why would he have to be? Didn't women just fall at his feet automatically? I had the sudden bone-chilling terror that this man wanted something he couldn't get from a date, perhaps my body chopped up in little pieces and arranged in neat white paper in the freezer. I shuddered at the thought and quickly tried to block it out.

Monsters aren't supposed to be beautiful. It's the rule. The Hunchback of Notre Dame was ugly. Frankenstein's monster was ugly. Nosferatu . . . ugly. Ugly was in the rulebook. And yet the man kneeling calmly before me wasn't ugly. Not on the surface. Look anywhere but into his eyes and he was the man women fantasized about from puberty onward.

He stood and backed away from me then, his gaze pinning me to the chair. He wasn't holding the knife in a threatening way, but he still held it. He started toward the door, then thinking better of it, he turned, came back to me, and pulled me out of the chair. I was almost to the begging point again, but he wasn't interested in me.

He stacked my chair on top of the one he'd been sitting on, folded the card table, and took the bowl and spoon.

I could have spent hours, days even, berating myself for not at least trying to run past him for the door, but I was glad I didn't. There was a combination keypad on the wall. Leaving required a retina and thumbprint scan. Whoever had me, had some discretionary funds. Maybe I was part of a secret government study.

The door shut loudly behind him, and I was alone in the cell with nothing but the clothes on my back. Concrete floor, concrete walls, unknown ceiling composition, all gray. A toilet sat in one far corner with no lid and there was an odd drain in the floor a few feet from the toilet. It was like prison without bars, or windows, or a bed.

I didn't know what time it was or why this mattered to me, but there was something disconcerting about not knowing whether it was day or night. When would I sleep? Not that it mattered. There was nothing to do but sleep.

In the movies, there's always a way out. It doesn't matter where the bad guy traps you, there's a way out. You can pick a lock, or use some kerosene, a match, and some sort of fuse and make a bomb to blow the door off. You can crawl out through the ceiling tiles, or smash a window, or find some weak point in the wall and start chipping away at it with a sharp tool you just happen to have in your pocket.

My cell was a fortress. It made the movies seem very contrived. It really isn't that hard to create an inescapable fortress if you stop to think about it. All you need is a solid floor, walls, and ceiling, and one exit using fingerprinting and retinal scans.

Two

I once read somewhere that predators conduct something called *the interview* with their potential victims so they can determine if their intended prey is worth the risk. Of course they don't call it *the interview;* that's criminal profiler talk.

I wondered if I'd been interviewed. I was known to give several talks a month. Had he been at one of them? Pulled me aside? Asked me charming, disarming questions? Pegged me as a lamb? A Red Riding Hood?

I didn't know. But surely I would have remembered those eyes. And if I hadn't seen him for the predatory animal that he was, I would have noticed his good looks. Would I have gone to dinner with this man if he'd looked at me a fraction less coldly?

I wondered how long he'd stalked me and how easy I'd made it. Had I been careless with door locking, thinking no one was watching and *just this once* it was okay? Had he been in my home, rifling through my underthings? Making a checklist of all the items in my cupboards?

I had a lot of time to think about these things but not that first night. After being left alone in the cell, I escaped to dreams. I could feel the drugs still swirling around in my system, so despite the circumstances, it hadn't been that difficult.

I dreamed about the luncheon, that he'd been there. We'd made eye contact, and he'd flirted with me. I don't remember if in the dream I flirted back.

When I woke, it took me several minutes to separate fact from fiction. Waking in the cell was the real nightmare. The dream had been so vivid. Colors, sounds, and smells more alive and immediate than I'd ever remembered them in life. I drank them up to hold onto them, somehow knowing it was the only sensation I would get for awhile.

The cell was kept at a steady temperature, never too hot or too cold. There was a vent in the ceiling, but it was too high to reach even standing on my toes or jumping. I stood under it a few days in a row, just waiting for some temperature fluctuation, anything that felt like something.

Everything was too constant here. The vent existed only to taunt me over what I couldn't have: a simple brush of air on my face.

The second day set up what was to be the routine. I'd been up for what felt like several hours, pacing back and forth. Part of it was the fact that I had no idea what was in store for me. This man held the power of life and death and everything else in his hands, and he wouldn't even make verbal threats I could psychoanalyze.

I decided this was by design. If he'd stalked me for any length of time, he knew how I craved social interaction. To speak to me would be to give me something he didn't want to give. Toward what purpose, I didn't know. If his intention was to drive me insane, he had a winner of a plan.

It wasn't until the second day that I noticed the lighting. It wasn't bright or super dim; it was this monotonous low illumination that stretched evenly over the ceiling. Like fluorescent lighting, but not quite bright enough for that. Maybe fluorescent lighting that had dimmed some. I couldn't begin to guess at the psychological makeup of someone who would buy lighting and run it constantly til it had dimmed to just the right level to torment me. Maybe that part was all in my head, and I was already going crazy.

Finally, I drifted to sit in one corner of the room, farthest from the exit. I pulled my legs up against my chest, resting my chin on them, and watched the door like it was going to do a trick. It was. Eventually it would open. Some part of me wanted it to because then at least whatever fate awaited me could happen and then be over.

When the door opened I changed my mind, silently begging for more time alone. My heart hammered in my chest so hard I was sure it was going to burst out. I took slow, measured breaths, trying to keep a level head. I'd considered rushing the door, but I had no chance of getting there quickly enough.

The door shut behind him with finality. That was it. Game over. That shot was gone. Not like I had any real shot, but when you're in no-win situations, you have to play this imaginary game in your head, the fantasy where you beat the bad guy and escape.

The bad guy stood watching me with a metal tray in his hands. For a moment, I imagined beating him to death with it. But then I was back to how I would get his finger and eyeball up to the keypad. Plus there was the combination. I could starve to death trying to figure it out.

He smiled at me—not a friendly smile—as if he knew exactly what I was thinking. He probably did. I'd always had an incredibly expressive face; it's hard for me to mask my emotions even under the best of circumstances. If I have a nice fantasy, my lips curl in a smile. If I'd done that, I was sure he knew what it meant, that I was running through various grisly murder scenarios that didn't feature me as the victim.

He crossed the floor and sat Indian-style across from me on the very edge of what I'd always deemed my personal bubble. Chicken noodle soup. Again. I stared at the bowl trying to determine what his game was. If it was time for breakfast, shouldn't he be feeding me something breakfast-like? Or was this another effort to confuse me on the time of day?

Did he seriously think soup was going to make me forget he had me locked up in what was basically a sensory deprivation tank? Or was this just a way to deaden the sense of taste so it was as deprived as my other senses?

He crumbled the crackers and lifted the spoon to my mouth. I'm not sure where my courage to speak came from. I was far past scared, but I was also angry, probably as much at myself for sitting and doing nothing as I was at him.

"I can feed myself!" As soon as I'd said it, I flinched. So much for bravery. I guess I expected him to hit me. Your average psychopath isn't known for his restraint. I braced an arm over my face as if it would stop any blow he decided to deliver.

Nothing happened.

With slow wariness, I lowered my arm. He sat mildly waiting with the spoon in his hand. I looked for anger in his eyes, but all I saw was calm, and the slightest tinge of amusement. I amused him. That made me angry enough to stop being scared again.

I wanted to lash out, fight. At that moment I didn't care if he killed me. I'd gotten it into my head that whatever he had in store for me would be worse the longer it took him to mete it out, and I saw no escape. If he killed me quickly, that would be better.

I was also more clear-headed than I'd been the day before. The drugs had worked their way for the most part through my system, and I wasn't so hungry I'd do anything. I cringed as I remembered letting him touch me through my clothing just to eat. There would be more of that and much worse if I didn't act now.

I slapped the spoon out of his hand and threw the bowl across the room. The glass shattered against the wall, breaking the silence. My mouth followed suit. "I don't want fucking chicken noodle soup! I want you to let me go, asshole!"

I was sure that would do it. Someone as anal as he appeared to be would snap under the strain of my rebellion. I was adorably naive. He stood with the tray in one hand, picked up the spoon, and left the room.

That was when it occurred to me how unbelievably stupid I'd just been. Yes, he was anal, and yes my little outburst would likely make him angry. But the amount of restraint he'd shown so far made me realize it was unlikely he'd offer me a quick death no matter how many outbursts I displayed. He'd spent too much time on this plan.

He was only gone a few minutes, but during those few minutes, I ran through at least twenty possibilities of what he might do next. He might starve me was one option. I'd managed to get some bravery due to the fact that I'm not usually that hungry when I first wake up, but starving wasn't something I wanted to do. I was reminded of this fact because I'd just the day before allowed him to fondle me once for each bite of soup.

He could kill me. A part of me wanted him to. It would be easier than living with what I would no doubt become if he kept to the same MO. He could have gone to get some dramatic implements of torture, or just the knife he'd used the day before to cut my bonds. I shivered at the last option and scooted back into the corner as if I could press myself through the wall to freedom on the other side. Maybe he would be quick about it.

The door creaked open again and my eyes shot up to meet his, terrified to see anger, but afraid not to know the status of my situation. He still had that calmness. He shook his head and grinned. If he hadn't been a sociopath, he would have been appealing. He had one of those boyish lopsided grins that tried to inch a little way up his face and made him look safe. It didn't fit with his eyes.

Instead of knives or guns or a million other nasty options, he had a broom, a mop, and a pail. He dragged a small trash can into the room behind him, and the door slammed shut again. I watched as he swept up the solid pieces of the soup and the glass from the bowl and dumped them into the trashcan. Then he mopped the floor, and without a word, took everything he'd brought into the room out again.

A few minutes passed before he returned to the cell; this time he wasn't carrying anything. He strode too fast across the floor toward me, causing me to cower in the corner like a wounded animal. He stopped just short of reaching me and crossed his arms over his chest. He looked like a parent disappointed in a child, as if I had been petulant and not within my rights and the bounds of normal human behavior to react in the way I had.

His cold gaze compelled me to speak. "I'm sorry." My voice trembled and sounded foreign to my ears.

Could this weak, helpless creature really be me? I'd spent the past five years giving speeches on empowerment and self-improvement and here I was, reduced to this. And so quickly.

I looked up at him, and he continued to regard me with something like interest. I could practically feel the violence curling within him, waiting like a viper to strike, but it never did. Instead, he stared at me as if he expected me to continue speaking. So I did.

"Please talk to me. Why won't you speak to me? Are you going to hurt me? Are you going to kill me? Please . . . "

He smiled. I don't know why I asked why he wouldn't speak. I knew why. It was becoming increasingly clear. I didn't know exactly why *me*, but I had a good idea why he wasn't talking.

He'd studied me, stalked me, knew everything about me. Human contact, speech, words, music. I needed stimulation. And he wasn't giving any of it to me. I was pretty sure he was trying to break me, and considering my lack of escape options, I was pretty sure he was going to succeed.

People always think they'll never break. They'll never give in. CIA operatives somehow crack, but not them. We live in this world where everybody watches so much TV, it makes them think they're superheroes. I'm strong, but anyone can be broken. I knew this. It's only a matter of opportunity, will, and persistence.

What prevents it from happening most often is most people sociopathic enough to break and condition someone properly don't have the level of self-control required to do it. Most with the control aren't big enough sociopaths. This was why I feared this man so much, not because I was his prisoner, but because I saw in him the blending of these qualities, which made the possibilities of what could happen endless.

He continued to watch me, cruel amusement curving his features, as if this was so much more fun than he'd ever anticipated the long nights he'd probably jerked off to the fantasy. Then he turned and left. The room felt quieter without him in it, as if his presence could somehow equal words for me.

Several hours passed, during which I paced the floor, and danced. I know that sounds insane. It *is* insane. It was day two, and I was flitting across the floor like a prima ballerina. But you don't understand how desperately I needed sensation, any sensation to make me feel like something rather than nothing.

When I was a little girl, I took ballet. I was pretty good, going all the way to acceptance at a major dance academy in New York. But in the end I decided against it. A ballerina's career is often over by twenty-five. By the time I was imprisoned in the cell, it would have been over for five years already.

I was glad I hadn't made a career of it. It would have ruined my feet. Although, I couldn't help but think ruined feet was better than being the prisoner of a sociopath.

So I danced. To distract myself, to move myself out of this plane of existence and into another, one where I was free. The cell was a perfect stage, plenty of room to *pirouette* and *tour jete* across it.

Even though the room was a static seventy-something degrees, I could feel the air move on my face as I whipped around and spun in circles. I felt my feet touching the floor with precision I'd never lost since giving it up. I heard the music in my mind as memories of old skipping records from the dance studios of my childhood played inside my brain.

I believed I'd won a round. I'd beaten the system he'd so carefully set up. When I couldn't dance any longer I sank to the floor. I was thirsty and getting hungry, but I wouldn't scream for him to feed me.

Screaming would have been normal; I knew that. But I'd already seen the way he didn't react when I'd smashed the bowl. Everything would happen on his timetable according to his wishes, and anything I did to try to goad him would make it happen that much slower.

Of that I was certain now. Besides, my throat was too parched to scream; it wouldn't help.

I didn't know when he would return with more food for me, or water, and I needed to conserve energy. Within minutes of my sitting on the floor in my corner, the door clicked open, and a bottled water was placed on the floor next to it.

It was cold, fresh out of the fridge, and I was profoundly, indescribably grateful for it. I was also suspicious. Had he been sitting outside the door listening to me? Were there listening devices? Something else? As I drank the water, I scanned the top of the walls.

This was an area I hadn't paid much attention to. After all, I couldn't reach the ceiling. What was the point of lying on my back all day analyzing it?

Then I spotted them. In the ceiling, at various points, were what appeared to be smallish black dots. On first glance, from the distance I was from them, they would look like random markings.

Pinhole cameras.

The son of a bitch was watching me. For all I knew, he had sound attached. He'd watched me dance and brought me water afterward. What the fuck did that mean? One thing was becoming clear, though. He'd entered the room three times since I'd been conscious. Each time I'd been sitting in the far back corner. That probably wasn't a coincidence.

If I was right, he wouldn't enter the room unless I was sitting in that spot. How could I use this information to my advantage? Obviously I had to eat, so I'd have to sit in the corner at some point, but I might be able to prevent extra unwanted visits by staying closer to the door when I wasn't hungry. Sleeping closer to the door was probably a good idea too.

Now I was back to trying to figure out the water. I had a clear enough idea of what was going on; thank you Psych 101. Behavioral conditioning and studies of Stockholm Syndrome had not gone to waste. Though I was aware that even with knowledge of what he was doing, it wouldn't stop him from succeeding, eventually. Or sooner, rather than later, since he'd known my weakness going into things.

I should have learned to be alone with myself, to not have to have noise or company or stimulation. I should have learned to meditate, taken up yoga or deep breathing practices.

I had fleetingly thought earlier about masturbating. I know that sounds wildly inappropriate. When you're in this sort of situation you don't want to do anything even vaguely sexual; it looks like an invitation. But it wouldn't have been sexual to me, not really. It would have just been comfort, stress relief, so I could avoid having a panic attack.

But there were cameras, and I knew it now. So no matter how much I wanted that release, I wasn't going to do it. It was tactile stimulation of the best kind, a weapon in my arsenal against the insidious plans already set in motion against me, but the risks weren't worth the payoff.

After I'd finished the water, I placed the bottle back beside the door and went to sit in the corner. I wanted to see if he was watching me closely enough to take the bottle right away, or if he'd wait. He was studying me, but I was also studying him.

I wondered if he'd tie me up to keep me from dancing, or doing yoga, or just plain moving in any way that had meaning besides mindless pacing. Tying me up would require violence on his part, something he didn't seem willing to bring into the equation just yet. Of course, he could always drug me again.

I stared at the empty bottle, my eyes widening. I couldn't remember if the safety seal had been on or not. I'd just unscrewed the lid and drank; I'd been too thirsty to think about it. Most mundane safety issues weren't concerning me right now.

Several minutes of paranoia passed, and I didn't feel myself getting sleepy. Finally, I relaxed and slumped against the wall.

I didn't remember falling asleep, but I knew I'd slept when the sound of the door creaking woke me. The dream had been loud and colorful, my subconscious mind flooding me with the sensations I needed to keep me reasonably sane, to help me hold out through my waking hours.

I panicked for a second, thinking I'd been drugged and tied up, but my arms were free. I was alert, and sitting up, watching him warily as he came into the room. I could smell the chicken noodle soup coming out of the bowl and found I was hungry, much hungrier than I'd thought.

He placed the metal tray on the ground and sat across from me in the same manner as before. He arched an eyebrow as if questioning whether I'd learned my lesson or not. Would I throw my food again and be sent to bed without supper? My mouth remained shut but my eyes told him I understood. Throwing the soup was pointless. It wouldn't result in a reaction; it would only make it longer before I could eat again.

He crumbled the crackers in and lifted the spoon to my mouth. It was still soothing, despite everything, a microsecond of safety and warmth in every bite, my mom taking care of me when I was sick. I tried to shut out those thoughts.

The soup wasn't for my benefit. It was for his, to more easily break down my defenses. The water had been the same. Small kindnesses. So I would come to trust and depend on him. I couldn't forget what he was, that I wasn't his guest.

I'd been afraid he would fondle my breasts again, but he didn't. Instead, every few bites he trailed his finger down my cheek. I fought hard not to flinch and equally hard not to lean into his touch. I tried not to react at all. I just sat there and let him do it, and then it was over and he was feeding me again.

Every few bites he'd do that same comforting gesture as if I were a wild cat he was trying to tame. As if he were rescuing me. Sometimes he stroked his hand through my hair, and once, in a moment of weakness, I leaned into the touch. It was stimulation, connection, communication. It was something. But every time I leaned in, I hated myself just a little more.

When the bowl was empty, he left the room. I sighed, leaning back against the wall, trying not to hold onto memories of his hand on me as if it were a good thing. A few minutes later, he was back, and I tensed again. Was this when it would start?

He held a strip of black cloth in one hand and moved slowly toward me. I struggled to my feet and backed away to a different part of the room. He advanced. Finally, I was backed into another corner and had nowhere left to go.

My eyes pleaded with him not to do it, but I didn't fight him. I didn't waste words because I knew he wouldn't answer them. I was shaking as he tied the blindfold around my eyes.

But I let him. I let him because I knew he'd do whatever he wanted anyway, and I was developing a sense of gratitude that he hadn't physically hurt me yet. He hadn't hit me, or cut me, or any of a million other things he could have done. He hadn't raped me, yet. And he seemed disinclined to do those things, at least in the classical way.

When the blindfold was in place, he took me gently by the arm and led me from the cell. We went down what I perceived to be a hallway, and he took me into another room, locked the door, then removed the blindfold.

We were in a large but plain bathroom. All decorations and pictures had been taken off the walls, if they'd ever been there in the first place. The mirror had been removed, and there was a faint outline on the wall where it had once hung.

There was a sink with toothpaste and a plain white toothbrush and a shower with a plain white curtain. On the toilet seat were clothes in my size: gray sweatpants and a white top that buttoned up like an art smock. No panties or bra.

There was a chair in the bathroom where he sat and regarded me.

"Please turn around," I said. I didn't believe he would do it, but he did. He turned his chair to face the door, as if he were a gentleman. I thought for a brief moment about wrapping my hands around his neck and squeezing, but I knew I wouldn't be able to kill him before he could break my arm.

I turned on the water, quickly shucked my clothes, and got under the spray. I drank in each sensation, the hot water spraying over my body, the floral scent of the soap and shampoo. After I'd finished, I rested my forehead against the cool tile and let the water run down my skin. I was afraid at any second he'd jump up and pull me out of there, but he didn't.

When I stepped out, I noticed he'd taken my old clothes away from me. Of course, I couldn't keep those. Those clothes would make me feel too much like a person. I slipped into the sweats and shirt, buttoning it quickly, and picked up my towel.

The towel was warm, fresh from the dryer, and it smelled like a spring meadow. Well, not really. It smelled like what we're told by the dryer sheet people that a spring meadow smells like. But I believed it right then. I resisted the urge to put the towel against my nose and inhale.

"Okay, I'm finished."

He stood and turned, giving me a once-over before replacing the blindfold. This time I was less afraid because it had become part of a routine, a natural continuation of actions before. He led me back to my cell and then was gone. That was the second day.

This pattern went on for seven days. I knew the time that passed because I used my fingernail to scratch a mark every day into the concrete behind the toilet. Three meals and a shower equaled a day.

He never tried to stop me from dancing. He must have known I'd eventually break anyway. There's only so much pleasure one can derive from even a well-loved activity when it's the only thing to do.

On the seventh day after my shower, he returned me to my cell. He removed the blindfold and stared at me, as if he could read my thoughts, or was trying to gauge his progress. He reached out and started to unbutton my shirt.

I pushed him away, but he didn't try to force me. He didn't start yelling; he did nothing but shrug and then turned toward the door. I panicked. I couldn't be left alone like this, in this endless routine of nothing.

"Wait. Please don't go." It had been a week. He showed no signs of releasing me. On the first day I'd been willing to trade groping for food. I needed to be touched now.

Dancing wasn't enough sensation, hot showers weren't enough. I had started to crave the gentle caresses that accompanied meals. I knew it was sick, twisted, but I needed to connect, to feel some sort of communication with him.

He stopped next to the door and turned toward me. There was something almost like pity in his expression. It was the closest thing I'd ever seen in those black eyes, and I wished suddenly that I could read his thoughts, so I'd know what to do. He pressed his thumb up to the fingerprint scanner.

"Please! Please don't leave me here. I'll do anything you want." I moved to him and reached out and touched him for the first time of my own volition. My hand gripped his arm; I couldn't let him leave me alone again. I couldn't keep up this maddening pattern forever. It had to stop, anything to make it stop.

My mind was going down trails I wished it wouldn't. His soul was ugly, but physically, he was beautiful. I could give in to that. I could let that touch me without feeling the need to vomit. And I wouldn't be blamed for it. I was the victim here.

He firmly, but gently removed my hand from his arm and walked me to the other side of the room to my corner. He shook his head at me, his eyes serious.

He turned again, and this time I didn't follow him. He left me alone in the cell, and I slid to the floor and cried.

THREE

Another week. That's what pulling away cost me. He didn't beat me or throw me down and force me; he just gave me another week. This time it was worse. It was worse because he denied me his physical closeness, touch.

For the next seven days he fed me three meals a day, chicken noodle soup, no deviation. I wanted real food and I was willing to do just about anything to get it. Soup is great, but three meals a day and it becomes less filling. You start to feel *full* but *hungry* at the same time.

He didn't come into the cell at all. He just opened the door and slid the tray in at regular intervals. He didn't touch me or physically feed me. I felt completely bereft. I couldn't believe I'd become so attached to my captor's presence until I experienced the absence of it.

The hot showers became a distant memory. Instead, once a day he'd send in a large pail of tepid water, a sponge, soap, and shampoo. And of course a clean towel and a new set of the exact same boring clothes he'd been dressing me in for a week. And a comb as well as a toothbrush and toothpaste.

Now the drain across from the toilet made sense. When I dragged the heavy pail to the corner to bathe, I was aware of how completely exposed I was. If he wanted, he could watch me clean myself, and he probably did. I was careful to ration out the water so I had enough to bathe, and also to wash and rinse my hair.

I'd stopped dancing. I didn't want to hold out anymore. I didn't want to hold onto whatever I could because I knew he was breaking me and succeeding. Dancing just made it take longer. I wanted to be done with it so I could move on to the next thing I would have to endure in his care.

Only in my dreams did I feel anything. I'd started dreaming about him, his hand on my face, feeding me. Even my subconscious mind had turned against me. Instead of dreaming in vivid bright colors and loud noises and vibrant tastes, I had begun to dream about the cell with him inside it.

My desires had shifted from wanting the outside world to just wanting him to come back into my cell and for my punishment to be over. I wanted to prove I could be better. I could obey and do what he wanted.

Finally, on the seventh day he stepped inside. He sat across from me as if nothing had happened, as if we hadn't had a period of non-communication for days, and he started to feed me. When he touched my face, I leaned desperately into his hand. I wanted him to be pleased with me, to know he could trust me now.

When the soup was gone, he took the tray away. I experienced a moment of panic, fearing I'd done something to upset him, that he would abandon me for another week, but he returned a couple of minutes later. He approached me and started to undo the buttons of my top. I didn't pull away this time.

. . . *She didn't resist as he* removed first her top, then her sweatpants. She stood naked and shaking, self-conscious. She wanted to cover herself but was afraid if she did he'd punish her again. So she stood there, looking down at the ground as he observed her. She knew he must have watched her on the video monitors while she bathed, had probably stroked himself to the sight of her. And yet, it was different for him to be so close.

He raised her chin so their eyes met, and he smiled. He was pleased, and she couldn't help the tiny flush of pleasure that went through her body at that idea. Then his mouth caressed over hers, an echo of everything he'd been from the beginning . . . gentle. As if everything he did, he only did it for her own good. To teach her.

She responded, her mouth hungrily accepting his touch. His hands drifted to her breasts, fondling her. She didn't think of pulling away. Instead, she thought of how she could get closer and pressed her breasts harder into his hands, her body screaming for more contact with his.

He put the blindfold over her eyes and led her to the door. She was terrified of where he was taking her. Were there others in the house?

She found she had little to worry about as he took her into another room. The combination keypad went off in a series of nondescript beeps, and then he laid her back on a bed.

She'd forgotten beds, what they were like, what pillows felt like against her flesh, or soft mattresses. She still wore the blindfold as he spread her legs apart, his fingers dipping into her and grinding against her heat. She was wet, so wet for him that she could hear it as his fingers pumped in and out of her in a chaotic rhythm. Then his mouth was on her sex, driving her on until she screamed.

"Yes, please, please don't stop touching me." Her breathing became erratic as she crested over the wave of her orgasm. Release, sensation, pleasure after so much nothingness. Then he was inside her, still gentle, thrusting in a steady soothing rhythm, like the ocean waves beating on the shore. She felt his release and then he pulled out of her . . .

I laid on the bed panting hard as the door clicked shut. The blindfold he'd used to transport me still covered my eyes. I didn't remove it. I was afraid if I did, he'd take me off the soft warm bed and put me back in the cell. I didn't want to go back there. If I had to be his whore to stay out of there, I would do it.

I had the sudden urge to cover myself, but resisted it. I refused to move one inch from where he'd left me. I would move when he allowed me to move and not before. I needed him too much to make him angry with me now.

Maybe half an hour passed before the door opened again, and immediately I could smell food. Not chicken noodle soup. Real food. He removed the blindfold.

Complete sensory overload.

There was roasted turkey, dressing, sweet potato casserole, corn, those great fluffy homemade yeast rolls. I dug into it as if I'd been starved, and in some ways I had been. Everything tasted so good, so much better than it normally did when I had these things at Thanksgiving. There was sweetened iced tea and a small plate to the side that had a warm slice of pumpkin pie on it. A can of Reddi Whip sat at attention waiting to cover the pie.

I was probably eating like a pig. He didn't seem to care, so I didn't care. He didn't appear to be conditioning me to have proper table etiquette. When he'd been stalking me, he'd probably watched me eat at dozens of functions, and this wasn't how I normally ate, the shovel-in method.

Once I'd convinced myself the food wasn't going anywhere, I slowed down and started to look around the room. The first thing I noticed was sunlight. I had a window! It was bulletproof glass (something I found out later) with bars over it. Still, it was a window. There were light, gauzy curtains to soften the starkness of the bars. The sun was shining, and the sky was blue, and I could see it. I knew what time of day it was, finally.

The room was lush with bright, rich colors, like those from my dreams. Fabrics hung on the walls and draped from the ceiling. It felt like being in a genie's bottle, only much roomier. There were several floor lamps and a few comfy chairs, the kind you could sink into and then have trouble getting out of.

Next to the window was a calendar with the date circled. June 3rd. It had been mid-May when I'd had my last speaking engagement. The room was even larger than the bad cell, and it had almost everything one could think of. There was a CD player and hundreds of CDs. There was an ornate desk and comfortable-looking swivel chair. A beautiful red leather journal sat on the desk with more pens than I could count. There was a clock on the desk that told me it was three-thirty in the afternoon.

One wall was all bookshelves with more books than I could read in a year. Scanning the titles I noticed some of them were old favorites of mine, and others were books I wanted to read but had never found the time. A few were books I'd never heard of but in genres close to the others.

He watched me as I ate and took it all in, then crossed to a small table, lit some incense, and put a CD in the player. Rich, classical music filled the room.

The bed I was sitting on was piled high with pillows and had a gold satin comforter on it that somehow didn't look gaudy.

When I'd finished eating, I cautiously got up. I was aware of and self-conscious of my nudity but I didn't dare try to cover up for fear he'd take everything away again. My feet sank into the softest, thickest carpet I'd ever felt, and I had to physically stop myself from lying on the floor and rolling around on it like a puppy.

On the far end of the room was a large walk-in closet, almost big enough to be its own room. The closet was filled to the brim with gorgeous clothes, all in my size.

"Can I . . . ?" I asked, reaching for a pair of designer jeans and a plum-colored cami top.

He nodded and crossed the room to open a dresser drawer to indicate bras and panties, all matching and from a high-end designer. I quickly dressed, trying not to let it upset me that he watched every movement I made. I'd just had sex with him. He'd touched and looked at every inch of my body. Now was a stupid time to be getting modest.

When I was dressed, I padded back to the closet to look at the shoes. There must have been a hundred pairs. I wanted to dive into them and try them all on, but not until I was alone again. Instead, I went through a few boxes until I discovered some silvery wedge sandals and put them on.

He watched me for awhile longer as I went through the room pawing through things, quietly ooohing and aaahing, momentarily forgetting I was a prisoner in a nicer cell. Then he got up and took the tray and silently went to the door.

"Wait," I said.

He stopped in the doorway and turned to me, his eyes questioning.

"Won't you speak to me now? Please? I did what you wanted." I cringed even as I said it. What he wanted had been to break me so utterly that I would beg him to rape me, and I'd followed his plan to perfection.

He placed the tray on the floor and crossed to me. Then taking me in his arms like a lover, he kissed me again on the mouth and left. I don't know what I'd expected. If he'd spoken to me I would have believed I could start bargaining. I could have read him better, dissected him.

If I could communicate with him in any other way besides letting him use my body, would I still so willingly allow him to do what he wanted with me?

After he'd left me to my own devices, I explored the rest of the room. There were two other doors, both without a keypad. I tried the first one, and it clicked open.

There was so much power in that moment. So much that I felt breathless with it. To put my hand on a doorknob and have it click open, to submit to my desire to go through it. It was almost more exciting than what was behind it.

A ballet studio.

The wall was lined with mirrors, though I couldn't bring myself to look too hard at my reflection. There was a closet with leotards and ballet shoes, all in my size. In one corner of the room nearest the door stood an old-fashioned record player and stacks of records, many I recognized from my time dancing.

There was a lot of Tchaikovsky. I thumbed through the records and put one on to play. I did a *tour jete* and then a *grand battement*. There was a fan in the corner of the room and Degas prints on the walls, perfect for spotting when I did turns across the room. I would definitely use the studio, but I was curious about what was behind door number two.

The same excitement as before hummed through me as I placed my hand over the second doorknob. There was a momentary fear it might be locked, but it clicked in my hand and relented as well.

It was a bathroom, and not just a bathroom. It was The Bathroom. The kind of bathroom you'd find in *Architectural Digest.* There was of course a toilet, sink, and a mirror. I practically ran to the mirror and wished I hadn't. My eyes looked too haunted to be mine.

Where did my soul go? I couldn't see it anymore. In the cabinet were piles of make-up, all in my brands and colors. Surely I could put enough of it on to hide the look in my eyes.

In the center of the bathroom was the king of tubs. A giant whirlpool, the kind that could double as a hot tub, if not a small swimming pool. There was a cart next to the tub filled to the brim with loofahs and bath gels, body scrubs and bubble baths. Unlit vanilla candles lined the wide brim of the tub, and a box of matches sat in a tiny tray on the cart. I could hardly believe I was allowed to take a bath anytime I felt like it. A bath. I could light the candles and soak in the bubbles, and read as long as I wanted.

A large shower stood in one corner of the bathroom, and next to it there were cabinets with stacks of fluffy bath towels, the kind so large you could wrap them around an elephant. And they all smelled clean and fresh from the dryer. A couple of white terrycloth bathrobes hung from hooks on the wall.

I went to the adjoining room and scanned the bookcase briefly before picking a classic and then running water in the tub. I poured some vanilla bubble bath in and lit the candles. I wanted to do everything at once. It hadn't occurred to me yet not to be happy.

I hadn't sat and thought about the fact that I should want out, not better accommodations. I was still his prisoner, still completely at his mercy and whims. He could take it all away at any second and put me back in that bare cell, that limbo. But I refused to think about any of that. Instead, I sank into the tub and turned the jets on and began to read.

I was in the middle of the third chapter when he entered the bathroom. I hadn't heard the door click open; I'd been so engrossed in that other magic place you go to in books. I dog-eared the page and closed the book, letting it fall to the floor and looked up at him.

The jets from the tub had made more bubbles, a false covering for the modesty I'd recovered after an hour in my new cell. He stood in the doorway naked and more beautiful than he had any right to be considering the circumstances. Since we were in the bathroom, and not in the bedroom where there was a keypad on the door and bars on the window, I could pretend things were normal.

I was his wife or girlfriend. He was rich—something obviously true beyond my fantasy life. He paid for everything while I did what wives and girlfriends of rich men did, pampered myself. I could pretend I'd given consent, that we had a relationship.

I wasn't sure if the music in the other room had gone off on its own or if he'd turned it off, but suddenly the only sound in the room was the water bubbling furiously around me, and my own ragged breath, part from arousal, part from fear.

He crossed to the tub and turned off the jets, and once again the room was cloaked in silence. I watched him cautiously as he got into the tub with me, disturbing the private sanctum I'd created because I'd created it with things that belonged to him.

The thought flitted through my mind that in some sense *I* belonged to him. I'd sold myself for pretty things, though at the time I had thought my price was much lower, since all I'd wanted was for anything to happen but him to leave me alone. For someone to communicate with me some way. Any way.

. . . *He slipped his hands underneath* the water to caress her skin and she let him. She knew she would either be his prisoner in a bare cell, or in here, these three rooms where she could pretend everything was okay.

His dark eyes drank her in as he pulled the drain on the tub. It took several minutes to drain out and while it did, he stroked her underneath the surface of the water. He dipped his fingers inside her and she found herself arching into his touch, grinding against his hand, begging for the contact that would get her off.

The water swirled away, leaving a mass of leftover bubbles. He rubbed her clit in light circles as she gripped his shoulders and whimpered against him.

"Please . . . " she said. She was sure she was begging him to stop, to not do this to her, let her keep her soul. But her body kept moving up to meet his touch, and some dark part of her feared she was begging him never to stop. Wetness pooled between her legs as the last of the water drained out and his hand started grinding harder against her while she panted.

He was beautiful, and he smelled good. He made her body hum with pleasure, and he gave her everything. She didn't have to worry about the things others did:

bills, jobs, social pressure. All she had to worry about was pleasing him.

She couldn't decide if she wished he would speak to her. On the one hand, if he chose to speak, his words could be cruel and demanding and her fantasy would be shattered. With only her soft sighs and whimpers as a background track, it was easier to pretend.

He ran his tongue over her belly and up between her breasts before latching onto one nipple. His grip dug almost painfully into her hip as he fucked her harder with the fingers of his other hand. He didn't let her come. Instead, he took her just to the edge, that maddening place when you'll do nearly anything to achieve release, when you are beyond the capability to reason.

He lifted her out of the tub and carried her back to the other room while she clutched at him, panting into the warm soft hollow where his neck met his shoulder. He set her down on her feet and wiped the bubbles from her body with one of the towels. Then, while she was still half crazed by the lust he'd created in her, he gently, but forcefully pushed her down to her knees.

The room seemed to narrow. It was suddenly too small, cramped, and claustrophobic. She wanted to scoot away, but he'd linked their hands in a mockery of love and he held her in place, patiently waiting.

He could take the fantasy away at any moment. All he had to do was yell at her, or physically hurt her, push her down and rip through her without regard for what tore or bled. But he didn't.

"Please . . . don't . . . " She looked up at him, wanting to find humanity somewhere buried inside his eyes, something to back up the almost civilized way he'd behaved with her. But he just watched her, and waited, knowing his lack of words took all of hers away.

She couldn't bargain with him, and so she bargained with herself instead. If she did what he wanted, things would go easier for her.

Her mouth latched around him and she sucked. He released her hands to run his own gently through her hair. Caressing, reassuring, comforting.

She'd had a boyfriend a few years before who had taught her how to deep throat. It wasn't a wasted tutelage because his breathing was getting heavier and louder. Then he came. He used one hand to massage her throat and help her swallow.

She wanted to die, but he wouldn't let her. He lifted her off the floor and laid her out over the bed. Then he held her wrists against her thighs and returned the favor.

Her eyes drifted shut and she pretended it was her boyfriend, back when she was practically a child and he'd held her down to make her orgasm. She thought about all the nights after when she'd masturbated and made herself come to that memory. And she writhed against the tongue of her captor and came again . . .

He let go of my wrists and went to the closet. I laid there, not daring to close my legs, trembling. He picked out another pair of designer jeans, and a black baby doll crop top and laid them on the bed, then he left me alone.

My hands shook as I put the clothes on. I didn't bother with a bra or panties, I just wanted to be covered, and I thought he probably preferred me without underwear. I hated myself for taking that into consideration even for a moment.

I was thirsty, but he'd thought of that. I hadn't noticed it when he'd carried me into the bedroom, but he'd brought me a large bowl of fruit: grapes, blueberries, strawberries, mandarin oranges, and pineapples. Sitting next to it on the side table was a bottle of water.

He was setting it up so he didn't cause me pain; I caused it. I caused it by rebelling. All I had to do was give in, submit in mind and body and I would never be hurt again. He'd see to my every need and give me the best of everything. He'd be better in bed than most men who take women willingly. He said it with everything he did, every touch, every caress, every physical pleasure he bestowed upon me. *Give it all to me. Give me your will.*

And that was when I knew. I had to kill him.

Four

I was falling too far, losing bits and pieces of my mind. If I didn't escape soon, I knew I wouldn't be able to. In the other cell there was no hope because there were no weapons. Now, I found myself surrounded with them. Not traditional weapons, of course, like guns and knives, but makeshift weapons that would do the trick.

Suddenly everything my eyes touched held a dark purpose. Shower curtain? Strangle him. Pen? Jab him in the throat. Lamp? Knock him out. I cataloged at least fifteen different ways to incapacitate him and then still more creative ways to finish the deed.

I couldn't let him live. He knew too much about me. He could hurt my family or friends, use them to lure me back. No, he'd signed his death warrant by taking me and even more so by giving me the tools with which to end him. He wasn't as smart as he thought. If he were, he never would have put me in the nice cell so soon, when I had some small piece inside me that was actually still me.

I've always been a squeamish person. The tiniest drop of blood freaks me out. It was the thing that had held me back. Besides my fear of not succeeding and being hurt or tortured to death for my crime, I was too squeamish.

Before, if I'd succeeded in killing him, I'd have to know the combination, then pop out an eye at the very least to get through the security. The fear of starving in a cell with a corpse had stopped me cold.

There were no pinhole cameras in the ceiling here. He must have thought I wasn't a danger anymore. He must have thought lack of dancing meant he'd broken me completely, that I was so desperate for his touch I would gladly stay in my pretty crate like a good dog.

He was wrong. I waited though, formulating my plan, calculating. I didn't want him to suspect, so I let the new routine settle in for a few days. I ate the fantastic food he brought me; I spread my legs for him, let him do what he wanted. I read and took bubble baths and painted my nails and tried on outfits.

I pretended I was okay. I was docile, submissive, pleasing. My eyes lit up when he entered the room, and I eagerly did whatever he guided me to do. Thankfully his tastes weren't too exotic. I'd gotten through the first times, and nothing had changed. I could handle it until I could make my move.

It got to a point where my acting became almost too good. I leaned into his kisses just a touch too eagerly, sighed a little too deeply when he brought me off with his mouth or fingers. I was falling for my own seduction. So it was now or never, while my desire for freedom and escape still meant something to me.

I still understood his touch wasn't the only touch in the world, and the pretty things he lavished me with weren't the only things in existence. There was still a world outside that room. So the fourth day in the new cell, the first day clouds darkened the window so the sunlight couldn't stream through, I was standing by the door, waiting.

I intended to kill him and run for my life, in case any other dragons guarded the castle. I had a pen and a sock in my pocket, and the heaviest table lamp in the room held in my hands in a death grip.

The lamp normally sat on the desk beneath the window, so his eyes wouldn't find it missing in time to stop me. I stood, tense, waiting. I'd decided his mistake was conforming too closely to a routine. He always brought my breakfast at nine am, according to the clock on the desk. It was no trouble at all for me to be standing crouched by the door at 8:55.

I knew I had exactly one shot at this. My intention was to hit him the second the door opened. Then if he fell forward into the room I could use the sock to keep the door from sealing shut, jab the pen in his throat to finish him off, and run for it.

The keypad clicked to life on the other side of the door. When people have these moments they believe are big, they often speak of time standing still, how it dragged on forever in slow motion. But for me it didn't drag. It was so fast I almost missed it. The door swung open and I pounced.

There was no time to be precise. The fraction of a second I took to aim, would be all it would take for him to stop me. I wasted no energy on that; I just swung out. His hand gripped my wrist so hard I knew if he twisted just slightly he could break it.

That was it. My big escape plan. And it was over before it even started. I searched frantically for something, anything to use as a weapon. It couldn't be over this quickly.

There had to be a way to beat him. He couldn't have shut off all my routes of escape. Criminals always made a mistake. Didn't they? Maybe his mistakes would never make a difference to me one way or the other. My sole source of help might be some random stranger noticing something shifty about this guy and following him.

I released the lamp finally, and it crashed to the floor. My eyes met his and instead of the anger I expected, they held disappointment.

Something inside me died.

If I didn't get out now I would lose myself entirely to the beautiful monster in front of me. I dug into my pants and pulled out the pen. He still stood partially in the doorway. If I could get past him before he stepped the rest of the way into the room, I could still escape.

The pen plan was even less successful than the lamp plan. I just wasn't fast enough or strong enough. I had a moment of absolute shame over that, shame that I wasn't a superhero, or one of those girls on TV that somehow manages to overpower someone three times their physical strength. Fiction had sold me pretty lies, and none of them did me any good now.

He moved the rest of the way into the room, and the door clicked shut. I knew he wasn't going to give me another opportunity like that. I'd had it and lost it. He released my arm and instinctively I backed away from him. The disappointment he'd had in his eyes was replaced by some indefinable hardness.

It wasn't quite anger. It wasn't human enough or uncontrolled enough to be anger. And he was always in control.

"I'm sorry. Please, I'm sorry. Please don't hurt me." I moved backward until the heels of my tennis shoes hit the wall behind me.

He calmly held his hand out to me, and I took it. What choice did I have? He led me to the door and then produced the blindfold from his pocket. I didn't try to fight him; I complied.

Whatever he had planned for me would be worse if I kept fighting. After the blindfold was in place, I heard the electronic beeps of the keypad, and then the door lock released. He took my hand gently and led me from the room. My arm still tingled where he'd gripped it to prevent me from hitting him with the lamp.

I was crying as we walked down the hallway. I knew he'd restrained himself from harming me. It was confusing to a degree I couldn't handle. It made me feel ridiculously and inappropriately grateful to him, and I knew that was what he wanted.

We didn't go far, so I knew we weren't going back to the bad cell just yet. In fact, I was sure we were next door. He closed the door and removed the blindfold. It was a plain gray room, much like my cell, only there were screens everywhere. Half of them showed the cell he'd kept me in originally. The other half showed my new suite of rooms. I didn't know where the cameras were exactly, what they were hidden in, but the point was they were there.

He'd known I was waiting for him with the lamp. I'd had no chance. Satisfied with my new understanding of reality, he put the blindfold back in place.

When the next door opened, I heard birds and felt a warm breeze on my face. He removed the fabric from my eyes and we were standing outside. The sun was starting to peek through the clouds.

I shouldn't have been shocked by what I saw. I'd seen something similar staring out the window of my room, but I just hadn't thought it would be like this on all sides. He linked his fingers through mine and led me around the house, as if we were lovers or friends, his grip never tightening or becoming threatening.

I could break the hold at any time and run, but to where? From the outside I could see my assumptions of his wealth weren't idle. He had money, possibly never-ending pots of it. The house wasn't a house, it was a fortress, a mansion. In another time, with slightly different architecture, it would have been a castle.

There were trees in the front yard and then what felt like a vast nothingness that stretched as far as my eyes could see. There were woods in the distance, but it was so far off I thought it might be a mirage. His house was situated on what felt like a grass-covered desert that seemed to roll on forever in all directions.

We could be literally anywhere. The driveway went on for what appeared to be several miles. And what then? He led me over to the large garage that housed his cars, plural. No surprise that there was a combination keypad over the door.

He released my hand and sat on the grass, staring up at me, that look of mild amusement on his face, as if to say: *what now?* What now was right. I spun slowly in circles trying to grasp how far out we were, the vast nothing.

If there had been lots of trees I could have believed we were close to a main road somewhere and I just had to find it, but we weren't. I wanted to run. I should have, but I couldn't help but believe running would make my punishment worse.

There was nowhere for me to hide, and without a car, nowhere for me to go. He wouldn't go to all this trouble just to release me. I fought with myself over what I should do. I'd been so ready to kill him and now, faced with such a long trek to even a deserted road, I was giving up?

I found myself walking down the driveway, toward the vast nothing that I hoped eventually would turn into something. I felt his cold eyes on me, sending a chill over my skin. I knew he was toying with me, and I was buying into it, but I couldn't just stand there or go back to my cell.

He was there, ready at every turn. He'd known I would try to kill him, and he'd been prepared. He knew I would do what I was doing now, and he was mocking me. But to react any other way would have been unnatural for me. It would be to give in. He won either way. It was a game stacked against me on all sides.

I walked until I was a good bit away from the house, if one could call something that imposing a house. I didn't look back. I was afraid to see him following behind me at some kind of perceived safe distance. Eventually I did turn back because I couldn't stand the way my stomach clenched at the idea that he was close behind me, playing with me and waiting to pounce.

He was still sitting there, casually in the grass. I was too far away now to see his face, but I could make out his shape. And then he stood. My heart dropped into my stomach. I imagined he was smiling, a hunter intent on outrunning his prey, though I was too far away to see his mouth to find the truth of this theory. He started to move toward me.

I turned and ran. I'd always been in great physical condition, but I couldn't run for distance worth shit. I just never built up that kind of endurance. It didn't take long before I was winded, and he was close enough for me to hear him running up behind me.

I couldn't outrun him; I knew it. I'd known it from the beginning, but if I didn't make at least the token effort I'd be beating myself up over it for as long as he let me live. If there had been trees, I could have zigzagged between them and hidden. It was just too open here.

His feet pounded closer and closer to me against the ground, dry and packed hard from lack of rain. Before he caught up to me, I stopped, turned around, and held my hands out in surrender. He stopped running a few feet from me and smiled that unfriendly smile, then nodded. Then he turned and started walking back toward the house.

I stood there for a moment, gawking after him. I wanted him to physically drag me back kicking and screaming but he wasn't doing that. He seemed so sure I'd follow. Well fuck that. He'd had me almost three weeks. I wasn't *that* far gone.

I stood defiantly with my arms crossed over my chest. He turned and when he didn't see me following right behind him, the smile left his face, and his eyes narrowed. He started to stride purposefully toward me, and I found my feet defying my desires and moving me back toward the house.

For all my tough thoughts, I didn't want him to hurt me. At root I was a coward, and I knew it. I didn't take enough risks, never had. I was just the kind of girl men like him dreamed of taking. The kind that was too afraid of pain to rebel in any meaningful way.

I'd stopped running because I was terrified of him knocking me physically to the ground. I was afraid if he did that, if he got a taste of violence toward me, he wouldn't stop. We were in the middle of nowhere, and he was my only hope. Keeping him from turning on me was the only thing that mattered.

He slowed his strides to match mine as we walked together to the house. If the situation were different, it would have been companionable silence. I didn't know how he managed the willpower to not reprimand me. But he'd managed the willpower to do every other completely calculated thing he'd done. So why not?

He was the most terrifying person I'd ever encountered, like a wild animal, and yet he reasoned.

Predatory animals are so frightening because you can't speak or understand their language. You can't reason with them.

As we got closer to the house, I kept thinking of the ramifications of its size. Surely a house that big, there had to be servants at some point. He couldn't possibly do everything himself. So people came to the house, and if they came to the house, I had a chance. If I screamed my head off someone would hear me.

He pulled out the blindfold, and I let him put it on me. When the cloth was removed from my eyes again, the fear I'd been secretly harboring was realized. I was back in the bad cell.

"Please, take me back to the other room. I'm sorry. I won't try anything again. I won't try to get away."

He skimmed his fingers lightly over my face, cupped my chin, and brushed his lips softly against mine. I leaned into the touch because I knew it was the last one for awhile. I hated myself for trying to savor it. I should be happy he wouldn't touch me, that I'd have a fucking break from his constant ministrations, but all I could think about was that I'd have to dance again in order to feel anything at all.

It didn't matter what I did or didn't do in that cell. I would be there until he thought I'd properly learned my lesson. He turned and left me alone, that deafening door click sealing my fate. Would it be a week? Two weeks? Surely a murder attempt, no matter how lame, would require more than one week's penance.

I pounded on the door until my knuckles bled, screaming and begging for him to let me out, to not abandon me again. I couldn't be alone like this again. Being in the cell now was worse than the first time. Seeing how bearable my imprisonment with him could be, and what I was getting instead.

I pushed down the feelings of shame at having displeased him enough to warrant punishment. Some part of me still knew it wasn't true, or thought it might not be true. I wasn't sure anymore, but I was starting to feel like I deserved the bad cell now.

He'd given me everything, and I'd tried to kill him. I finally moved back to my corner, cradling my injured hands. I soaked in the stinging feeling because it was something, and it let me know I was still real.

Not long after that, the door opened. My usual bathing necessities were slipped into the room, along with a tray with bandages and ointment for my hands.

"Thank you." I couldn't stop the words. And somehow I knew any attempts at escape now were just denial and an unwillingness to accept reality.

I scooted the pail of water, soap, and bandages to the drain and first worked on my hands. I was sobbing by the time I'd finished bandaging. It was like that moment when you know you're going to die and it's too late to do anything about it. You just have that sickening knowledge that that's what's about to happen, that apprehension.

I knew what had happened, I just couldn't stop it. I wouldn't scream for help; I couldn't. Not anymore. I couldn't scream because he was taking such good care of me. He'd gotten me bandages.

The rest of the day I didn't make a fuss. I did what I was supposed to do. I ate my chicken soup, and I slept in my corner. I scratched off a day into the concrete behind the toilet and ran my fingers over all the other days I'd spent there.

I don't know why I still hid the marks. I knew he watched me and had probably at some point caught me doing it. But he'd ignored it. He didn't seem to care about my crude calendar. I repeated the date over and over again in my head because it was important for me to know what day I was on.

When I slept that night I dreamed of the good cell, bubble baths and music, rows and rows of books and CDs, blush pink nail polish, and fuzzy slippers. And I dreamed of him. His eyes boring through me, seeing all my secrets, his hands on my body, and his voice whispering in my ear.

When I woke up, I was bleeding.

FIVE

In the master bathroom of what I had come to call *the good cell*, in the cabinet had been tampons and pads. Both. I hadn't thought anything about it at the time. If I was going to rebel and potentially fail, I should have thought about it and picked another date.

Now I was stuck in a bare cell bleeding like a stuck pig. It was disgusting. Still, he didn't change the routine. Whenever he opened the door I begged him for something. All he had to do was go down the hall to the bathroom and get it, but he didn't acknowledge my request. Instead, he let me bathe twice a day.

Finally, I stripped off my clothes and went about the cell naked. I knew he did it just to punish me. Feminine protection in his book was a luxury not a necessity.

I spent a lot of time in the corner thinking, trying to analyze my captor. I wondered what his background was. Surely he had to understand psychology at least a little to be able to do this. Maybe he was some type of quite literally mad scientist, using me as a study in behavioral conditioning.

That's the thing about conditioning. You can know it's happening all you want; it doesn't change the results. Eventually you break, reduced to something less than human. I felt like an animal as I crouched in the cell, blood dried on my leg. I felt wild.

I reacted like an animal. I found I listened for every little sound, watched every movement he made. I read body language and communicated through touch more than I had in my entire life. I spoke to him, mostly when I was scared, begging. But I hadn't spoken any words of substance in over three weeks.

He opened the door again and brought in my food. It was the first meal since I'd decided to hell with clothing. I wondered if he would be repulsed by it, if he was the type of man who was deeply disturbed by a woman's natural cycle. But he seemed neutral on the matter.

I spoke then, not my normal begging or pleading, but something more meaningful. I wanted to fight this degradation of communication and not forget how to talk.

"Are you a scientist?" My voice sounded strange to me when it came out at a normal volume and pitch, not through tears or panic.

He had been on his way out the door when he turned sharply toward me, his face shocked. It seemed to unbalance him that I would bring up casual conversation at a time like this.

It made me bolder. In my time as his prisoner, not once had I ruffled him even the tiniest bit. He'd expected everything I'd done, found it amusing and predictable, and now I had done something he found surprising. A part of me was afraid I was digging my hole deeper, but another, much larger part believed I might buy myself reprieve from my punishment if he found me sufficiently interesting. So I kept talking.

"You aren't shocked by anything I do, except maybe this. So I wondered if you'd studied it. I studied it in college. I was originally going to be a psychologist specializing in research, like this, only . . . more ethical."

His lips quirked up in the least disturbing smile I'd witnessed on him so far. Still, he didn't speak to me. But he didn't leave me alone either. He sat on the ground a few feet away, watching and waiting for me to continue.

I wrinkled my nose at the soup and crackers he'd put before me. God, I wanted the real food again. I'd do anything for a steak and a baked potato. I crumbled the crackers in and started to eat. I wanted to touch him, wanted him to touch me, but I knew if I made any move toward him, he'd leave again.

"Instead, I ended up getting my degree and writing self-help books of all things. But then you probably know that." A pause. "Why did you take me?"

No answer.

"Do you hate women?"

No answer.

I took another bite.

"If you talk to me, I'll still do whatever you want. I'll still let you touch me."

His eyes darkened; I'd crossed the line. He stood and went for the door.

"Wait. Please. I'm sorry. I won't ask for anything. I know you have your reasons, okay?"

He turned and nodded at me once, then sat beside the door. The distance he'd put between us wasn't lost on me. I took a deep breath and then a few more bites, chasing it down with water. He wasn't leaving, and so I felt brave enough to ask what had been on my mind for awhile now. Getting my period had reminded me of more than just basic survival, but biological realities.

"Are you going to kill me if I get pregnant?"

No answer.

My voice shook a little as I spoke. I wasn't crying, but there were tears in my voice, that catch you get when you start to get emotional but are holding back the floodgates.

" . . . Because I know you can't just take me to the hospital. And I don't know if you have anyone you can bring in . . . or if you would even want me then. Please, I don't want to die. I was on the pill before. The prescription is in my purse. You can put me back on it . . . "

He shook his head.

I took another bite, and more water to try to calm down so I could talk without going into blubbering sobbing fits. "No? You *want* me to get pregnant?"

He shook his head again.

"Are you sterile?" God, I hoped so. These were genes you didn't want to spread. I didn't want to give birth to another sociopath.

His eyes were cold as he stared at me. As far as he was concerned, the question and answer portion of the day was over. But I could see in his eyes I'd figured out the truth, and I felt relief wash over me. One less thing to worry about.

I finished my food without speaking again as he watched me. I didn't know what else to say. I wasn't sure what more he could take from me, but I knew he'd think of something if I pushed too hard. As it was, I wasn't sure if I'd be in the cell longer now because of speaking.

When I finished eating, he took the tray and brushed my hair out of my face with his fingers. I leaned into him. I was ready to do anything he wanted, just to let me out.

The cell was bad because there was nothing to do, but it was worse because it meant *I* had been bad. I'd displeased him, and that was starting to matter to me. I'd fought the desire to please him, but I couldn't help it. I knew what he was doing to me, but it didn't change how I felt, how I longed for him to touch me.

"Please, take me out of here," I whispered, as he ran his fingers through my hair. "Please."

I stood, and he kissed me. I moved my arms around his neck, but he gently took my wrists and moved them down by my sides. Then the kiss was over and he was leaving again. He turned away, and I felt the panic bubbling over.

I'd made no progress. I'd just been a diversion, but it wouldn't affect anything. What if he never forgave me for trying to kill him? What if he never let me out of the cell?

"No . . . please don't leave me. I'll be your whore. I'll be whatever you want, please."

I heard him punch in the combination code and then the click of freedom I couldn't have, and he opened the door. He turned and smiled at me, the smile of victory. Then he let the door shut softly behind him.

Several days passed, the bleeding stopped, and I was still in the cell marking off the days. He'd supplied me with clothing again and my bathing supplies, but I chose to remain naked. I wasn't sure if this was considered disobedience, but I was counting on his self-control slipping, that at some point he wouldn't be able to stand not taking what was bare to his gaze.

But if it fazed him, he composed himself before entering my cell. He brought my food and bath stuff, looking at me, but nothing more.

On the seventh day I expected it to be over. I'd done my time, surely he would touch me again. I would let him, and then I would be rewarded and get to go back to the good cell. The room where I was favored. But day seven came and went without him making any move toward me.

I hadn't built up the nerve to talk to him again since that one day. I was too afraid to change the routine. I wasn't sure exactly what sins had mounted against me and if speaking was one of them.

I needed touch, comfort, something. I was losing my tenuous grip on sanity, on reality. Everything felt fuzzy, and sometimes I wasn't sure if I was awake or asleep. I prayed it was a nightmare, and I'd wake up back in the good cell again. I'd stopped dreaming of escape because every part of me knew it wasn't possible. My subconscious mind chose to spare me the torment of dangling carrots I couldn't eat.

Instead I dreamed of the good cell, something I had some hope still of achieving. As the days slipped onward, I began to doubt I would ever get to go back there. Maybe what I'd done was so bad he could never forgive it.

I'd hoped being in the cell naked would entice him to come to me, that he wouldn't be able to resist taking what he considered his. But nudity alone wasn't cutting it. In an act of sheer desperation, I laid on my back in the middle of the room so every camera saw me. I spread my legs and touched myself. I didn't know if the cameras had sound attached, and I wasn't sure if I was moaning for his benefit or because I couldn't help it.

It had been more than a week since I'd had an orgasm. In the short time I'd been in the good cell, he'd brought me to release so many times it made my head spin with it. Now as I stroked myself, I realized how much I missed the pleasure he gave me.

I was in the middle of possibly my third orgasm when the door came crashing open. Everything inside me said to stop. Run. I had no idea where I would run to, but instincts usually operate on the run principle.

Instead, I boldly met his eyes, my fingers slipping inside my pussy, daring him to respond in any way. I didn't care how. He could fuck me or beat me. Any touch, any response from him would be welcome. But he stood there, his black eyes penetrating me, refusing to give me even anger in a physical manifestation.

He slammed the door behind him, and I stopped and moved to the corner. My heart was beating practically out of my chest, as slow dread started to creep over me. I'd wanted a reaction but now I was terrified I'd gotten one. I didn't need him out of control and angry.

My desperation had made me stupid. Minutes ticked by like months, and then finally the door clicked open again. He brought in the things for me to bathe, and clothing. When he left it was the first time in longer than I could remember that I was relieved he hadn't touched me.

I bathed quickly and put on the clothes. As I picked up the shirt, a book fell out. I backed away from it like it was poison. Was it a trick? I knew I didn't get nice things in the cell. Or was it like the bandages? I didn't know which was the correct thing to do, ignore the book or read it.

I slipped the sweatpants on and buttoned up the white top while staring at the new variable. The fabric felt weird against my skin after walking around so many days without clothing. Clothes made me feel like a person, and as a person I couldn't deal with what I'd become. If I remained a naked animal, it was better, easier. But he was finished making my life easy.

After circling the book a few more times, I picked it up and moved back to my corner. The corner was the only spot that held comfort because I knew if I was there, there was a chance he'd open the door and come for me.

I blushed, recognizing the book's title as something I'd read once in a much different time and place. I cracked the spine and started reading, knowing the contents would arouse me despite everything, but also knowing that if I didn't read, I might never achieve absolution from my captor.

It didn't take many pages before I noticed the first place a highlighter had been used over the text. The word *master* glared back at me in bright sunshine yellow. At the next instance of the word, it was highlighted again. I flipped through the book to see hundreds of bright yellow rectangles. He'd probably stayed up an entire night doing it. Or spent days on the project, hacking away at it chunks at a time.

It was a book I'd once read and gotten off on, and I still got off on it, only now, it was true. A true story about me. Reading it made me ache to touch myself again, but I didn't. I knew he must be watching, and I didn't want to be caught again. I'd been in the bad cell for two weeks. Much longer and I wasn't going to be able to hold onto any of my sanity.

The book was a slim volume, something that could be read in a few hours if you didn't dog-ear the pages and stop to masturbate. Within minutes of finishing it, I heard the key code being depressed on the other side and the door opening. He hadn't come with food, though I was hungry, and for a minute my pulse pounded at the idea that he might be there to take me back to the other room.

He approached me and stopped a few steps away from where I stood waiting in my corner. I moved my hands up to the buttons of the white artist's smock. He shook his head at me, and I let my hands fall to my sides.

He started to leave. What the hell did he want?

"Please . . . don't leave me here."

Normally he turned at least to look at me, but this time he didn't acknowledge my voice. Instead, he punched the numbers into the keypad. I wasn't ever getting out of there.

Then I knew what he wanted from me. It would be obvious to any thinking person.

There was a time when it would have been difficult, if not impossible for me to say the words, but I was desperate and I hadn't lied when I'd said I would be anything he wanted me to be.

"Master, please."

He'd gotten as far as opening the door, and he stopped, letting it fall back and latch shut. Then he turned toward me, a slow smile spreading over his face. *Yes.* That was what he wanted. I was getting out.

Adrenaline hummed through my veins. Whatever it took, I was getting out.

He crossed the floor slowly, and then he was unbuttoning my shirt.

. . . *She leaned into him as* he removed her top and cupped her breasts, pinching her nipples painfully. In the time before, she would have cried out at the sensation. Now she was just glad to be getting sensation at all, even if it hurt. His mouth latched onto her breast, and her breathing deepened as he swirled his tongue over her flesh, soothing where he'd just hurt her.

She gripped his shoulders as he stripped the sweatpants from her body. She never wanted to wear these clothes again. He pushed her to her knees; she fumbled with the fly of his pants. Then she was sucking him, desperately seeking to please him enough that he would forgive her for her former sins.

He stroked his fingers through her hair, comforting her, urging her onward, and then he pulled out of her.

"Did I do something wrong?"

In response, he positioned her on the concrete floor on her hands and knees facing away from him, spreading her legs slightly. She could hear him rifling through his pants on the floor, and then he was on his knees behind her.

His fingers found her clit, and he stroked her. She moved back, trying to grind harder into him. It had been so long since he'd touched her like this. She was willing to do anything to make sure he never stopped for so long again. She panted, and a moan escaped her throat.

"Please . . . yes . . . " she whimpered.

He kept going until she came and screamed out her release, sobbing with relief that he was finally touching her again. Then she turned to see him squirting something out of a tube.

Lubricant.

She started to crawl away from him, back into her corner. "No, Master, please."

He shrugged, then stood and moved toward the door again. He refused to give her the peace of doing anything without her permission, no matter what a joke it was. She panicked.

"Don't leave me here again. I can't take it. I can't take anymore of this. I've been here two weeks, please."

He turned back to her and held up the lube, a question in his eyes.

She nodded and moved back into the position he'd placed her in. She still wasn't sure this would earn her a ticket out of the cell, especially since she'd fought him.

She couldn't help tensing when he approached her. He stroked her back over and over, his fingertips playing lightly over her skin. "Shhhh," he soothed. "Shhhh."

She began to calm. He'd refused for weeks to speak to her, and although this wasn't exactly speech, it was communication. It was sound. She began to cry over the tiny crumb he gave her and relaxed further.

He prodded her entrance with one lubed finger, as he continued to stroke her back with his other hand. She didn't resist. She cried out as the finger eased inside her, and he went more slowly, more gently.

She found she was grateful for that. It was small, but it was something. He continued with the one finger until her body got used to the sensation, and the burning pain ebbed away. Then he repeated the process with two fingers while her fear mounted higher.

"Shhhh," he soothed again, when she started to cry, his free hand rubbing her back.

When her body had gotten used to fingers he withdrew them and slowly eased his cock into her. She let out a hiss, but soon the pain passed, and he urged her to start moving. Slowly, she fucked herself on him as he panted behind her. Then his fingers returned to her clit, and she began the climb toward her second orgasm.

When she came it felt like a shot of electricity zipping up her spine. He pulled out of her and cradled her in his arms, stroking his fingers through her hair and kissing the top of her head while she cried. More from relief than anything else . . .

Six

He didn't take me to the good cell. Instead, he led me to another room, one I'd never been to. When he removed the blindfold, my mouth fell open.

Too many things to look at. There were chains on the wall and a metal table with cuffs on it. There were whips and canes and other various implements of pain that I didn't exactly know the names of. There was a giant, round bed with a red velvet comforter pressed against one wall, beside which another set of chains dangled. There was a black leather couch in the center of the room and a box overflowing with more sex toys than I'd ever seen outside a retail environment.

I realized what I'd done too late. I'd accepted. I'd called him *Master* and accepted he was in charge of me, not me. Before that moment had I still had freedom? I wasn't sure.

He would have left me in the cell probably forever. But which was worse? The cell? Or the new tortures waiting for me in this chamber?

It was a testament to how much of me he'd taken that I thought the bare cell was worse. He wouldn't leave me alone in this room. He would be there with me. It should have sickened me. It should have made me scream in terror, but all I could feel was relief.

I wasn't sure if I'd ever see the nice room again, but this was better than the past two weeks of nothing. I turned to see him gauging my reaction. The door to this new chamber, equipped with the same technology as the others, stood open.

He always gave me choices. Or maybe what he gave me was force wrapped in the pretty package of pretend free will. I'd spent a lot of time analyzing him, and though I knew he was obviously in some sense crazy, there was always a logical basis for his decisions. He believed he was giving me options, in his own twisted way, and therefore he wasn't the bad guy.

Either he didn't recognize blackmail wasn't a choice or he didn't care. He hadn't used physical violence. Until now. Whips seemed pretty violent to me. But I knew him now, more intimately than he thought.

He believed he could hide his soul from me by never speaking, but his actions told me everything I needed to know. He wanted me to beg for the whip. And I would do it. I'd do anything he wanted. The door stood open, and he stepped aside, and we danced our little dance.

Would I run? Or would I stay and obey him? The choice was obvious. There was nowhere to run to. He'd already shown me this was true. He would never force me to do anything in that dungeon room. He would just put me back in the bad cell and ignore me like a crated, misbehaving puppy.

His eyes held challenge, and I stupidly still had enough defiance inside me that I wouldn't run from him because I couldn't face the shame and humiliation of going to that other cell again. The last incarceration had been two weeks, no time off for good behavior, no response to any of my demands or clever tricks. Next time would it be three?

Or would he tire of this constant disobedience and shut me away forever?

I didn't move toward the door. I held his gaze and said, "I'll do whatever you want."

I could see evidence of his arousal outlined through the pants he'd put back on. He was wearing only jeans, the muscles of his chest so beautiful I could hardly stand to look at him.

Still, he didn't move. I walked to the door and shut it, and then panicked because I'd just locked myself into a sadistic torture chamber with my captor. My captor who I trusted not to hurt me because he never had before, not physically anyway.

I'd made my choice. I turned and moved back toward him, still naked. He hadn't put the clothes back on me, and I was glad. I'd rather be naked than wear the clothing I'd come to associate with punishment.

I watched him, waiting for his next move. He studied me for a few minutes as if his brain were cataloging all my actions and reactions on a hard drive somewhere.

He held his hand out to me, and I stepped forward and took it, trying to stop shaking. He smiled that soulless smile that made me feel warm and like I was dying all at the same time. A flush crept over my body from the predatory gleam in his eyes.

. . . *He led her to the* bed and arranged her on her knees facing away from him. The soft velvet was a warm caress against her skin. She heard his footsteps recede over the concrete floor, and she squeezed her eyes shut, not wanting to see what he'd gone to get. She was unsure which would be worse, an instrument of pain, or pleasure.

When he returned, his hand was gentle on her chin, raising her face toward him, and she opened her eyes. She could see something soft and almost human in his gaze, and she wanted to latch onto it. He turned her face so she could see the riding crop dangling loosely from his hand.

Her eyes flew back to his as the same cold fear she'd had in the other cell came rushing back. His eyes held question. He'd only hit her if she agreed. The mockery of her free will made her angry, but her anger was dwarfed almost completely by the feel of his hand on her face.

He'd been gentle in the other cell. He'd taken something profoundly scary and been kind and reassuring. She was still reeling from the careful way he'd held and rocked her afterward and then watched her with something like concern as he'd put his pants back on.

Her eyes drifted to the riding crop again, and she nodded. Then he was behind her. She tensed as she heard the crop slice through the stillness of the room. It was deafening. And then the sharp, loud pain. She gasped, tears in her eyes.

"Please . . . "

He stopped.

"No, don't stop." She wished she could take the words back, but any further begging died in her throat as she relaxed and let the crop fall on her.

How had she allowed him to turn her into something so ugly? Someone who craved any sensation at all, even if it was pain. A few moments passed, and she let the rhythm of the strikes wash over her. When she'd reached the threshold of complete surrender, the pain morphed into something tolerable and almost . . . pleasant?

Her body betrayed her, taking this new sensation and responding with arousal.

He stopped then, and she had a moment to catch her breath before he returned with a single-tailed whip. She'd thought it was ending, but he'd only been warming her up for more. She'd read enough to know this wouldn't be pleasant.

The whip cracked a few feet from her, and she jumped, finding her knees no longer wanting to support her weight. He allowed her to lie on her stomach and ran his hand over her back and the roundness of her ass. Then the strip of leather whipped across her skin, leaving a sting so sharp it brought tears to her eyes.

As he whipped her, she cried out but didn't beg him again. She let it happen, whatever he wanted, as long as he didn't take her back to the bad cell.

He continued, and she found herself floating while the endorphins flooded her system, and he pushed her higher still. Tears streamed uncontrollably down her face, but it wasn't the pain that made her cry.

It was release, absolution. The surrender, finally, of everything to him. The acceptance that she was now his creature, not her own, and the inexplicable peace that brought her.

Finally, it stopped and she could feel a warm wetness on her back. He'd made her bleed. She felt his tongue trailing over the opened flesh. He stepped away from her, and she worried he wasn't finished yet. Maybe he would take her beyond her ability to tolerate the pain to make her prove her new loyalty to him.

When he returned, he had a small basin of water, cloths, bandages, and ointment. He patched up her wounds, then turned her in his arms and kissed her softly on the mouth.

He retrieved the blindfold again and she scooted back.

Her voice cracked, "Are you taking me back to the cell?" If he took her back there and left her to rot after this . . .

He shook his head. She crawled back to him so he could tie the piece of fabric over her eyes . . .

When the blindfold came off, I was in the nice room again.

"Thank you, thank you, thank you."

I couldn't stop saying it. It was a mindless litany now. I turned in his arms and my mouth found the hollow of his throat, and I kissed him.

He left me then. When he returned, I was stretched out on the bed, the pillows propped underneath me, watching for the door to open again. He rolled in a cart laden with barbeque chicken, corn on the cob, fresh green beans, cole slaw, rolls, a salad, iced tea.

He sat across from me and fed me. It was the first time in a long time. I let him, leaning into his touch each time he stopped to stroke my breast. I no longer saw this as what I had to give him in order to eat. Now it was reward.

Anything that wasn't the bad cell was a reward. In less than six weeks he'd turned me into this. I hated the part of me that was so weak I couldn't hold out longer, that I'd sell my soul for him to touch me and not leave me alone.

Wouldn't any sane woman be grateful to just be left alone? What was wrong with me that being kept in that cell without his presence was the worst thing he could do to me? Far worse than being his fuck toy.

I'd convinced myself it would have been different if he'd been as ugly on the outside as he was on the inside, but he wasn't. He was cruel beauty, a sculpture, a god, and I couldn't tear my eyes from him. I'd seen his expression soften in the dungeon with the whip. I'd do anything to have him look at me like that again, no matter how insane he was.

It didn't matter anymore because we were both insane. How can the crazy judge the crazy? He was a sadist, and he'd trained me into the perfect masochist. Or maybe it had already been there, waiting for the right circumstances to present themselves.

I'd been thinking more about my first boyfriend and how I'd reacted to being forced to orgasm, how different I was from those around me.

He'd finished feeding me.

"Did you pick me because you knew I would respond this way?"

He just smiled.

"You've got money and looks, and you're obviously smart," I said. I left off the crazy part because I'd just promised myself I'd do whatever I had to do to stay in the good cell. I wasn't even sure this wouldn't buy me more isolated punishment. Still, I pressed on. "You could have anyone you wanted. You could have seduced me, and I would have willingly played your games."

He arched a brow at me, and immediately I realized how stupid that sounded. He *had* seduced me, after a fashion. He didn't want the illusion of control; he wanted *actual* control. That was something very different. No matter how women might fawn over him, what he wanted, what he needed, was something he could only get in this way.

He pushed me down onto my back, and I stayed there. The thin gashes from the whip burned from the pressure, but I didn't move. He wasn't finished with me yet; he'd just taken a break to feed me. Now he wanted a fresh and unmarked canvas to play on.

He took the cart out of the room. I knew he was coming back for me, and whatever he was bringing with him, I would submit to it because I couldn't go back to that hollowed-out cell. I needed to be surrounded by things, distractions, amusements.

I needed to lose myself dancing in the studio, or reading, or taking hot bubble baths. I wanted to soak up every physical sensation I could, in case it was all ripped away. All of it was an extension of him, and therefore all of it was a way in which he touched me.

He returned moments later with a long red taper candle, matches, a vibrator, and two bowls. He filled one of the bowls with water, then returned, arranging everything carefully on the table.

. . . *He placed one of the* chairs at the foot of the bed and pulled her to the end so that her legs dangled over the edge. She held her breath as he lit the candle and tilted it inches above her stomach. A hiss of air escaped her lips as the hot wax landed a drop at a time. A sharp stinging burn, that ebbed as the circle of wax dried and hardened.

She jerked as if by the movement she could escape the pain, and the first few bits of wax dried in long slivers. He shook his head at her and peeled the strips of wax from her body, dropping them into the empty bowl. He rested his hand firmly on her stomach.

Her voice came out barely above a whisper, "You want me to be still?"

A nod.

He removed his hand and let another drop of wax fall from the candle. He held it close to her skin, and she felt the warmth from the flame before the burning wax hit her flesh. A tear rolled down her cheek, but she didn't move. The wax dried in a little round dot. She let out a shaky breath, and he repeated the action.

Over and over. She closed her eyes, focusing on breathing, crying, but not screaming because it might cause her to move. The little burning points of wax were being left close to one another, as if a pattern were forming on her skin, but it was so gradual she couldn't make it out. There was a puff of breath as the candle was extinguished, and she let out a shaky sigh.

She heard a buzzing and then he'd shoved the vibrator inside her. Her muscles clenched as it pulsed through her. She remained still, afraid of disobeying him until he took her hips and coaxed her to move and respond to the vibrations.

The pain was forgotten, but then he lit another match and was dripping the wax over her nipples, continuing to encourage her to move. He'd worked her into a frenzy, but she wasn't so past rational thought she didn't know what he wanted from her.

He wanted her to come while he hurt her. The idea both repulsed and excited her as her body pushed around and reinterpreted the pain from the wax. She screamed as she came, her eyes shooting open. He snuffed out the candle and laid it on the little table, then pushed the vibrator deeper inside, holding it in place, forcing her to come for him again.

He pointed to her stomach and she looked down. Where he'd wanted her to remain very still, she saw he'd spelled out a word with wax. *Mine.*

She nodded, "Yes Master, I'm yours."

The verbal surrender was just one more piece of her that now belonged to him. He carefully flecked the pieces of wax off her body and dipped a washcloth into the bowl of water. The water was cool as he gently dragged it over her skin.

He wrung the cloth out over her belly and chased the trails of water with his tongue. She watched as he stood and retreated into the bathroom again. She lay there, her legs spread wide just as he'd positioned her, as the vibrator pushed her toward another orgasm.

He returned a few moments later and withdrew the toy.

"Please . . . no . . . I need . . . " She was babbling. She'd been so close. She shut her mouth and looked away from him. He'd already made her come several times that day. What was wrong with her that she needed more? She didn't care how she ached for it, she wouldn't beg again.

Her body jerked at a new sensation and she looked down to see him back in the chair, a razor and the bowl of water in hand, shaving her. She was so sensitive. It was maddening to have the razor gently brushing her skin so close to her clit.

When her pussy was bare, he ran the cloth over her sensitive flesh. She arched up to meet him, a small whimper leaving her mouth. He wrung the cloth out again, letting the droplets of cool water trickle down her slit.

Then his wicked tongue was licking up the drops, dipping inside her, and lapping at her clit. He held her ass cheeks with his hands, pulling her up to him, as if she were a banquet he couldn't get enough of.

She came for him again, moaning "Master," because it was the only name she knew. He slid up her body and into her, pounding her into the mattress.

She screamed.

"Please," She didn't want to go back to the cell, but the way he fucked her, with her back still raw and hurt, was too much. "Please let me be on top." She was too afraid to say *no.*

He stopped, concern on his face, as if he'd gotten caught up and forgotten her back. "Shhhh," he whispered, and flipped them so she was on top.

"Thank you." She rode him, and he gently stroked her back until he came inside her . . .

He went to the closet, then he tossed me a pair of jeans and a black T-shirt that said *bite me* in bright red letters on it. I found I was disappointed that he hadn't. I dressed and sat on the edge of the bed, unsure of what I was supposed to say or do.

"Master?"

He looked up.

"When you whipped me back there . . . was that . . . punishment?"

He shook his head slowly, his eyes burning straight into me. I swallowed hard. I'd suspected as much. The cell was punishment; the whipping was because he enjoyed it. Got off on it.

"I'm sorry for what I did that day," I said quietly. I didn't have to elaborate.

How did one apologize for attempted murder? Or was it self-defense? I couldn't be sure anymore. I only knew that I'd tried to kill him and instead of doing to me what I'd attempted to do to him, he'd spared my life.

The only physical violence I'd experienced at his hands, I'd allowed him to do. A bargain, an exchange to keep me out of the cell and win his good favor. I was starting to feel safe with him. He'd gone from being just my tormentor to being my tormentor and protector, though I needed protection from nothing but him.

He simply nodded in response to my apology.

"Are you still angry with me?"

He looked confused, and it occurred to me he hadn't been angry. He'd probably expected I would lash out at some point. It was natural in my position to do so, a part of the dance of victim and victimizer, and I'd played my part predictably.

He'd probably looked forward to the moment he could show me the futility of my efforts to escape. To break me just a little more. No, there had been no reason for him to be angry. It was just one more success. The cell had been punishment for disobedience, plain and simple. Anything else I'd read into it was wrong.

He picked up a hairbrush off the vanity and I flinched, thinking for a moment he might beat me with it, not out of anger but out of some sadistic need he had that he was slowly beginning to let me see. But he sat behind me instead, his legs coming around on either side of mine, and he brushed my hair. Slow, gentle strokes. I closed my eyes and relaxed.

When he'd finished, he kissed me softly and left. He returned moments later, handed me a notebook, and was gone.

SEVEN

I didn't pick it up at first. If the last book he'd left for me was any indication, I wasn't sure I wanted to know its contents. Instead, I left it on the table and went into the ballet studio to stand in front of the mirror.

I lifted the T-shirt over my head and gingerly peeled back the medical tape. I couldn't stand not knowing how bad the whip marks were. I didn't know why it mattered. Even if it wasn't deep, he could just be getting started. And I didn't know whether he'd let me heal before he did it again. I waited until I'd gotten the bandages off before I dared to look at the damage. I pulled my hair up and peered over my shoulder at my reflection. It wasn't that bad. The bandages on the ground didn't have much blood on them, another good sign.

It looked like he'd stopped as soon as he'd broken the skin. He'd also been careful to only hit my upper back and shoulders, nowhere it would cause permanent damage.

I glanced up at where I knew the cameras were and wondered if I'd get in trouble for removing the bandages he'd spent so much time on. But if he was going to do it again, I thought it needed air, so the cuts would close more quickly. I tossed the bandages into a garbage can in the corner.

I looked back into the mirror, this time at my stomach, at the light red burns left by the candle wax. I traced my fingers over the letters of the word *mine*, the temporary brand that I never wanted to fade away. Then I slipped the top back over my head, wincing as it settled over my skin.

I'd accepted he was never letting me go. He'd invested too much time and money in all this. I couldn't begin to guess how many months he'd stalked me to discover so much about my likes and dislikes. If he hadn't taken me in the way he had, I would almost think he was a regular guy trying to impress me with gifts. But I knew that was ridiculous.

He was a predator and I was his prey. No matter how much I came to depend on him and crave him, I wouldn't forget that. What he'd done and was continuing to do to me was wrong, but the constant struggle to fight it based on moral fortitude was too emotionally exhausting for me. Acceptance was easier.

If I wanted to keep any part of my mind intact, I had to obey. There were only so many trips to the bad cell I could handle before I lost it completely, before I became a shell instead of a person. The good cell told me everything I needed to know. He was offering a gift I was fortunate to be given. He was offering to let me keep enough sense of self to not fall into madness.

He didn't have to give me the nice room and the studio and bathroom and all the luxuries these rooms held. He didn't have to give me a window or the best southern food one could put in their mouth. He didn't have to ever give me any kind of pleasure. I tried to hold onto the reality that it didn't make any of it okay, but I was having a harder time seeing that because my reality had been narrowed to him and the things he could make me feel.

I hadn't looked through all the CDs or books yet. In the short time I'd been in the rooms before attempting to kill him, I'd spent most of my time in the studio or taking bubble baths and trying on clothes. I thumbed through the CDs finding a wide range of things I liked: classical, rock, jazz, some international music.

I wasn't a fan of international music and wondered if he was including his tastes as well. But I was curious, so I slipped a Middle Eastern CD into the player. The music was rich and earthy and alive in ways no other music I'd ever heard was. It pulsed through me, steady drum-beats, layers upon layers of rhythm and music.

The room contained no TV or DVD player, no computer. There were no movies, no news, no commercials, no Internet. Nothing to link me too closely to the outside world. No faces to see but his, not even on a screen. No voices but my own calling out in the silence.

I looked more closely at the books. I was familiar with the shelves at eye level. They held a lot of my favorites, but now I was looking more closely. On the lower left-hand row, closest to the dresser, almost as if it were hiding, was a complete section of erotica. Something like fifty titles. All of them were the same theme. Kinky. Most of them Master/slave fiction. A few of them familiar.

Story of O, for example, was a classic that I would just as soon not read again, given my current circumstances. I didn't know how many things from these books we'd be acting out. And I wasn't sure I wanted to know.

It was one thing on paper, in a fictional world; it was quite another when it was real. Still, the books were there, calling to me, tempting me to read and be reawakened to their erotic secrets.

I was no longer the teenager giggling under the covers with a flashlight reading something naughty and bad. I was a grown woman living it, and some darker part of me was clawing to get out because what choice did I have left but to give in to the dark?

My eyes drifted back to the table and the plain black spiral notebook, like a college student might use. I knew it wasn't empty. It wasn't a blank book for me to write in. That I already had, and I'd been writing in it.

No, the notebook contained information. It was his first explicit communication to me, and I was terrified to find out what it contained. After weeks of existing in a state where I had to read nonverbal signals, I was afraid to get actual words from him.

I was scared to see how much of him I knew, and how much of him I didn't. But I couldn't ignore it anymore. Whatever was inside, I needed to read it, to prepare myself for what was coming next.

I picked up the notebook and took a bottle of water from the mini fridge before lying down on my stomach across the bed.

The book held no mention of why he'd taken me or for how long he intended to keep me. Though I knew the second answer: forever, or until he grew bored with me. I was afraid of what would happen once he did grow bored with me. Though I determined reasonably that could be a long way off, judging from his obsessive and meticulous behaviors so far. A man who plans for months before taking a slave doesn't grow bored with her in the same length of time.

Instead of explanations, the book contained rules and punishments. Much of it I'd figured out already with regards to punishment, but to see it in black and white only confirmed my suspicions and left me no excuses to disobey and then claim ignorance.

As I'd already known, obedience would keep me in his good favor and in the rooms I presently occupied. I had suspected as much . . . and yet there was always the fear he might move me back to the bad cell on a whim. But he'd written on the crisp white-lined pages that he wouldn't as long as I tried to submit, and I trusted him to keep his word.

If I'd learned anything over the weeks of my captivity, it was that obedience equaled reward, and disobedience equaled punishment. He never lashed out in anger. He was always in control, both of me and of himself. It made me put faith in him that ultimately, if I followed the rules, he wouldn't harm or kill me.

Masturbation wasn't allowed for any reason. Sexual pleasure would come from him and him alone. He mentioned the erotica. He wanted me to read it, at least one book a week, but I wasn't allowed to touch myself. If I did, I would be punished.

Punishment was as I thought and as he'd confirmed earlier with only a look. I would be sent to the cell for any infractions. Each incarceration would be longer than the one before it. There was no sliding scale based on the level of disobedience.

I had expected the murder attempt would land me in the cell longer than if I'd just tried to escape. Or that trying to escape would offer me a longer punishment than if I'd refused to obey some small whim of his. But it was all the same.

Saying *no* offered the same level of punishment as trying to take his life. The next time would be three weeks and then four. Eventually I could end up withering away in that cell if I didn't obey him.

In some sense he offered me freedom if I wanted it. All I had to do was refuse him and he wouldn't touch me. I would have nothingness and food that no longer held flavor, but I would be free of his touch.

I knew I'd never take that offer because the freedom he offered me was the kind I'd always loathed. My mind was too full and in need of stimulation to be locked away in the cell forever.

The extremeness of the punishments ensured I wouldn't rebel. I'd already decided I would do anything he wanted without question because I didn't want the cell, and I never wanted to look at chicken noodle soup or crackers again.

I had no doubts he could follow through. If the wait became too long for him, he wouldn't shorten my punishment. He'd kill me or take another slave before he broke his own rules.

He could already have other slaves and I'd have no way of knowing it. It would explain the ease with which he could resist me while I was being punished, despite his obviously strong sexual desire otherwise.

His entire fortress-like home could be a camp for slaves. The thought sent a white-hot bolt of jealousy through me.

I knew it was an inappropriate response. I shouldn't feel jealousy that someone else might call him master and spread their legs for him. I should feel pity for the others he might have taken.

Twenty pages of hand-written text was all it took to specifically lay out the rest of my life for me. There was no room given for interpretation. If he made me come, it was reward. If he whipped me, it was reward.

Any attention or physical contact was reward, no matter the nature of the contact. It was almost appalling to see it written out for me so plain and naked. But I'd already known it. I'd arched up toward him as the riding crop had bitten into my skin, and I'd been thankful to have something instead of nothingness. I'd gotten wet from his gentle ministrations as he'd cleaned and bandaged the wounds he'd inflicted on me.

I was his now beyond safe denial. Beyond right and wrong.

The rest of the notebook contained protocol, daily rituals and the words he wanted to fall from my lips. My training was about to begin in earnest.

He left one more meal for me that evening and brushed my cheek lightly with his fingertips. He lifted the back of my shirt to inspect my skin.

I tensed, wondering if removing the bandages was considered disobedience, if I would earn three weeks for something so simple and small. My body shook from fear that I wouldn't have the chance to prove I could obey him.

"Shhhhh." He left a gentle kiss on my back, and then he left me alone with my food. I cried with relief.

The next morning my alarm went off at seven-thirty. He would be there at nine. I went through the list, doing what he'd laid out in the notebook, preparing myself for his arrival. I didn't leave anything out because I knew he'd be watching from the dark room with all the monitors.

I bathed in the bath oil he wanted, wore the makeup he wanted, fixed my hair the way he wanted. At nine o'clock I was in place, exactly as he'd instructed, smelling of jasmine and waiting.

. . . *The door opened and he* walked into the room, already undressed, his erection swaying as he moved. She was naked on her knees with her legs spread wide. Her hands rested on the floor on either side, her palms facing up in supplication.

The lines in the sand had been drawn, and it was real now. Before, she'd had the small comfort of not accepting. Holding onto some tiny internal piece of her own identity, some vague hope of escape or rescue.

For weeks in her mind she'd thought only of appeasing him for survival, to hold onto herself, so she could think of getting away. Now she was his. The smile on his face said he knew it too. His patience had paid off.

He stood in front of her and her hands went around to grip his ass, pulling him toward her, as if all she wanted was for him to fill some part of her. She wrapped her lips around his cock and greedily sucked him as he ran his fingers through her hair.

He pulled out of her suddenly, and she whimpered.

"Did I do something wrong?"

In reply, he pulled out the blindfold. For a moment, she couldn't breathe. All she could think was that she'd missed something. She'd said or done something wrong. Maybe she'd bitten him without meaning to.

"No . . . please . . . " She scooted away from him until her back hit the bed. He arched a brow at her, standing like a Greek statue, the scrap of black fabric draped over his hand. Reluctantly she crawled back to him, the tears sliding down her cheeks, and then everything was darkness as he secured the blindfold and led her from the room.

She nearly fainted as her bare feet touched hard concrete floor. He removed the blindfold, and she collapsed to the ground. It wasn't the bad cell. It was the dungeon.

"Thank you, Master," she whispered.

He crossed the floor to the mini fridge and returned with a cold bottle of water. He twisted off the cap and handed it to her. She drank and didn't stop until it was half empty. He sat on the ground and held her.

She wasn't sure if she imagined the concern in his eyes. Maybe she saw what she wanted to see. She acknowledged she was his, but it didn't mean she wasn't aware he was a monster. He couldn't feel anything. He seemed to be waiting on something, an explanation.

She was sure in his mind he felt he'd been magnanimous. In some ways it was true. And yet she couldn't imagine being more afraid of him if he'd beaten her on a daily basis and cut strips of flesh from her body with a razor blade. He must know how completely he'd broken her.

"I was afraid I had done something wrong and you were taking me back to the bad cell," she said quietly.

His eyes hardened, and once again she was looking into the emptiness she'd seen on her first day with him, all softness erased. He hadn't been about to take her back there, and she'd opened her stupid mouth and perhaps given him reason to put her there now. All she could think was: three weeks.

She'd nearly lost her mind after one week, and thought she would die after two. She couldn't do three. She'd find some way to end her life if he took her back there.

"No, Master, please. I'm sorry. If I've upset you . . . please please don't take me back there." She stroked his cock . . . placating. She bent to replace her hand with her mouth, but he pushed her off him and left the room, slamming the door behind him.

He returned several minutes later and threw the notebook down on the ground in front of her, his finger jabbing at the page. In furious pen scribblings he'd circled a passage and underlined the words within it. It was a page about punishment:

You will be punished only when you willfully disobey me. As long as you try to submit to my wishes, you'll be safe.

The words *willfully disobey*, and *try* had been heavily underlined. She swiped at the tears on her face and looked up to see his outstretched hand. She took it and followed him to the bed. He placed her on her knees away from him, pushing her down so her forearms rested on the dark velvet, her ass raised in the air.

She tensed when she saw the lubricant. The last time he'd been gentle and made it exquisitely pleasurable. This time, however, he didn't seem intent on starting small. He lubed his cock and then, as if there could be any doubt, he washed his hands in a little sink beside the row of whipping implements.

He nudged her opening, and she fought to relax. Slowly, inch by painful inch, he filled her, and she cried out. He waited and allowed her to adjust to him before moving in and out of her.

He pulled her body up so she was arched impossibly back and cupped a breast with one hand while the other dipped between her legs, pumping in and out of her in rhythm with his thrusts inside her ass.

When his fingers were slick with her juices, he removed them and pressed them into her mouth. In a wild frenzy, she sucked, and lapped up what he offered her before his fingers returned to pumping inside her, and then to her mouth again. Over and over he repeated the action, feeding her as she moaned around his fingers.

He slammed into her as he came and then let her fall back down onto the bed, her legs quivering jelly. She lay there, shaking and waiting, knowing he wasn't finished with her.

His fingers thrusting into her, combined with his cock in her ass had taken her to the very edge of release. But she didn't come.

He pulled out of her, grabbed her ankles and flipped her onto her back. When she looked at him, he pointed behind her. The chains on the wall. She bit her lip and nodded. She'd never liked being restrained, but he wasn't asking her permission. He was asking if she'd learned her place, if she would accept it and let him chain her with no fuss or if he'd have to put her back in her cell for awhile longer so she could think about it.

The metal locked against her wrists, then around her ankles. She hadn't noticed the ankle chains before. They were bolted into the floor and had been under the bed out of sight until now. The chains spread her legs wide.

He pushed a long, thick vibrator up inside her and set the vibrations to the lowest setting, enough to make her throb and whimper but not enough to bring her release. He crossed the room and rummaged through a small closet until he found what he was looking for, a professional-grade camera.

He circled the bed, taking photographs of her, but she didn't care. She couldn't care. She was too far gone and desperate to come. In the back of her mind she feared he'd send the pictures to people she knew or post them on the Internet, and yet still she mindlessly thrust her pussy up at him, trying to buck against the vibrator as if by doing so she could make the pleasure come faster or harder.

He used a roll of film and then placed the camera on the ground. His hand wrapped around the end of the vibrator and fucked her with it so hard she was breathless. With his free hand he gripped her throat, his cold eyes meeting hers.

"Master . . . " Her voice was pleading, but not pleading to be let go. Pleading to come.

He released her throat and for a moment she believed he thought she was begging him to stop.

"Please, don't stop. I want to come . . . please."

Her cries were unnecessary; he wasn't unchaining her and letting her go. He moved the vibrator to the highest speed and unchained one of her wrists, placing her hand on her breast, encouraging her to rub herself. Then he loaded another roll of film into the camera and the shutter began to click again.

She came, screaming and bucking as the camera flashed. He walked over and kissed her on the forehead and then left her alone in the room. He hadn't bothered to remove the vibrator. It still pulsed inside her at the highest speed, causing another orgasm to build.

When he finally returned, she'd climaxed five more times and was so wet, the vibrator would have slipped out if not for her free hand holding it in place.

He removed the toy and shut it off. It was dripping with her cum. He held it in front of her face, and she obediently opened her mouth and sucked it as he slid it in and out, until it was clean of her spendings . . .

When he returned me to my room I knew why he'd been gone so long. He left me to go prepare my breakfast as I stared at the walls. He must have had his own dark room because there were large blown-up photographs on the walls. Photographs he'd just taken.

I tried not to look at them, but I couldn't seem to tear my eyes away. I went to one wall and ran my fingertips over the picture. My legs were spread so wide, straining against the chains, the tip of the vibrator sticking out, my wetness glistening against my legs, and my face a cross between pleasure and torment.

EIGHT

Days bled into weeks and then into months, and then it was fall. The leaves were falling off the trees ushering us into winter as I continued marking off the days on the calendar.

Five months.

The first day forever ago when I'd been waiting for him on my knees was the turning point. Everything changed for me after that. I could still form coherent thoughts but all of them circled around how to please him. To make him smile at me. To get his eyes to soften when they looked into mine. The photographs on the walls taunted me. Over the months, a few more were added, some replacing Degas prints in the studio. Something about me changed in those photos. The first series he took still upset me sometimes because there was such a mixture of pleasure and pain.

He wouldn't let me forget what I had been and what I'd become at his hands. He wanted me to see it like he saw it.

By July, the photos had changed, like they weren't even me. Pain was dwarfed by pleasure, even when there were lash marks on my back, even on the occasions when there was blood. Whatever he did, it didn't matter. I wanted it all.

I should have been repulsed by him. Intellectually I knew that was the proper response. It was the victim response. It was the response that would say to the world I wasn't broken, even though I would have been in more pain that way. It was a mercy to be broken, to be his to the point that it was what I wanted.

If I hadn't been reshaped and reformed into the docile little pet he wanted, I would have cowered and cringed away from him and screamed and cried. Sometimes I screamed and cried anyway, but only when the orgasm overtook me so strongly I could do nothing but empty my soul onto him.

I'd been out of the bad cell for months. I never went back there again. A few times I came close when he'd introduce something new and scary, but ultimately I obeyed whatever he wanted.

After awhile it stopped being about the cell and that perceived punishment. It became instead about him being disappointed in me. I only cared about his eyes and how they reflected me.

In the good cell the warm throbbing between my legs was almost constant. It didn't matter what I was doing. Dancing, bathing, painting my fingernails. Because whatever I was doing, my thoughts rarely strayed far from him and memories of the last time he'd touched me. If I had been his obsession, he had become mine just as strongly.

Sometimes I imagined that when he left me in my rooms, when he was finished playing with me for the day, he went out with his friends and laughed and talked. Maybe he didn't think about me at all. Or he watched television and wasn't troubled with thoughts of me until some small mention, no doubt getting shorter and farther apart, would come up about my disappearance.

I had this image of him as some sort of almost Patrick Bateman from *American Psycho*. That he lived a double life. One side all privilege and creamy soft-white business cards with perfect fonts, the other blood and darkness. Monster and man.

I found myself wanting the monster because it was honest, a level of honesty most go their entire lives without confronting, always content to hide behind their social masks and business cards.

It was October. By now everything was about him, but at the same time I missed Halloween. The costumes, the parties, going out with my friends. Friends I'd forgotten, as if they'd died. I couldn't see their faces anymore when I closed my eyes; I only saw him. That intense beauty that was almost painful to look at.

My fear had become so entwined with my arousal that I craved everything he did now. I could stay here forever. I wanted to. My family and friends, my career and colleagues, they were all shadows to me now.

I had the barest notion there had been police investigations, frantic searches, tearful panic over my going missing. I'd been a blurb on the national news, a tragic case of a young woman with a bright future and loyal fans. The speculation that a crazed fan had taken me, or someone who hated me.

Which category did my master fall into? Either? Neither? I'd never know. I'd long given up the hope he would ever speak to me.

But he didn't have to use speech. Every touch, every caress, every lash of the whip, crop, or cane. It was all communication, a private conversation that no one else could intrude upon. Before, my life had only been words, shallow, meaningless words dripping from my mouth with no real content. Words for the sake of words to make me feel less alone in the world. But I had been alone.

Completely.

Then he took me and filled my world so much that even without words, I wasn't alone. We were connected now so deeply that to lose him was to lose life itself. He was everything. We communicated on the primal level of touch. Dominance and submission. Master and slave. Nothing else was required.

I woke on the morning of Halloween with a vague sense of loss. I thought it was because of all I'd missed this year. Or because we were approaching the holidays, and suddenly time would have more form as I lost my first Halloween, my first Thanksgiving, my first Christmas and New Years, but that wasn't it.

My alarm went off at 7:30 as it always did. I happened to glance over to find the door standing open.

I can't describe in any rational way the panic that surged through me. What the hell was this? I hadn't felt this way since the first day of my imprisonment when the blindfold had covered my eyes in that still silence, before I'd seen his face or felt his hands on my body.

Normally, he left me instructions with my last meal of the day for what he wanted the following day. I should have known something was wrong when he didn't. Maybe I had. Maybe that was the gnawing feeling that had crept inside me.

I bathed in jasmine oil and got ready. At nine o'clock I was on my knees a few feet from the door, waiting for him. That's when I looked up and noticed the keys. On a little table next to the door were a set of car keys.

If I took them, would the garage door be opened? Would I press the little button and hear the beeps to indicate which car? Could I leave?

That should have been my thought process. My thought process instead went: *Is this a test? Does he not want me anymore? Is he abandoning me? How can he abandon me? I did everything he wanted. How can I mean nothing to him after he's trained me like this?*

I didn't love him; he didn't love me. But I was his. I belonged to him. That had to count for something. I was addicted to the way he touched me, the contrast between pleasure and pain he always delivered to me. Violence and gentleness. I couldn't get enough.

I didn't care how I'd arrived at this point. The only thing that mattered was that I was there, and I never wanted to leave. I was his willing slave, evidenced by the fact that I only looked at the keys briefly before my eyes went back to the floor, and I waited.

Nine-thirty came and then ten. Ten-thirty and I hadn't moved from the spot. I was getting hungry. There were snacks and water in the mini fridge, but I didn't move. I didn't want to. I didn't want him to find me not where I was supposed to be.

Finally, just before noon he stepped into the room. I didn't look up at him. I kept my eyes on the ground as he'd trained me, despite my desperate desire to look into his eyes to find what was there.

Then he was standing in front of me, his feet in my line of sight. I wanted to reach out and touch him, but I refrained. I wanted to beg his forgiveness for whatever I'd done to upset him, but I didn't. I just stayed where I was, my breath coming out in heavy pants, anticipation thrumming through me for his touch, any touch.

I didn't have to wait long. He gripped my chin and forced my eyes up to meet his. He was angry, and I didn't know why. Finally, I spoke.

"Master, please, whatever I did to upset you, you know I didn't mean it."

Had I ever seen him angry before? Truly angry? No, I couldn't remember a single time over the past months that I had. He'd been so restrained. Everything so calm and orchestrated. Everything following his plans, even my lame attempts at disobedience.

Now seeing him angry unhinged me, and I found that old fear creeping back again. Not the fear mixed with the arousal until I writhed and panted beneath him. This was more uncertain fear.

Had he snapped? Was he broken too? What the hell was going on? He turned away from me, standing stiffly, his breath suddenly matching my own previously heavy panting.

He wore only jeans, and I could see the tension of his shoulder muscles as he forcibly restrained himself. From what? Killing me? Beating me?

He'd whipped me many times. I had a few scars which I knew would stay with me forever or as long as he let me live, but he'd never whipped me out of anger. It had all been out of desire.

Finally, he seemed in control of himself. He crossed to the closet and after a few moments returned, tossing a pair of blue jeans and a pale pink T-shirt at me . . . and the silver wedge sandals where the ribbons tied around my ankles.

I put them on. Had there ever been a day when he hadn't come to me in some way? Was he tired of me now? Early on I had feared this day, waking in cold sweats over it. The day he got bored with me. The day he killed me. Now I couldn't work up the emotion for it. I just didn't want it to end.

How was it possible, given our circumstances, that he could tire of me before I tired of him? He tossed me the car keys and left the room. He was serious. A thousand thoughts ran through my mind, all whirring through my head at the same time, so I couldn't separate one of them out.

I sat dumbly still as if it were some kind of trick, that last tiny hope that it was a test I could still pass. My mind refused to accept just yet that passing meant leaving him.

Moments later he appeared in the doorway again, an annoyed look on his face. He came back into the room and wrapped his hand around my arm, jerking me through the door, pulling me through the house.

The blindfold was no longer covering my eyes, no longer segmenting the rooms into disembodied pieces of a larger whole. Now, seeing it all at once, the house was even more impressive inside than I'd always imagined it to be. And yet . . . it was only him.

No servants. Had he given them the day off so he could get rid of me? Did they just come in on alternate days? For a moment, I had this crazy thought we were the only two people left alive on the planet.

Perhaps the servants were keeping to the shadows. Did they know what he'd done? Did they care? I held onto the wild hope that he didn't want to be rid of me. No, some servant suspected, and he was making me leave so they wouldn't find me. But that didn't make any sense. Why would he set me free on the world? To hide the evidence, wouldn't he have to kill me first?

I stumbled a bit, and my ankle twisted under my foot. Stupid wedge sandals. These weren't the shoes for women with tiny ankles. I cried out and he turned, the smallest shadow of concern on his face before he masked it again and was back to the business of expelling me from his house.

We were in the entry hall, the front door just feet away. He seemed to have every intention of throwing me out onto the lawn and leaving me to my fate with the elements if I was too stupid to use the car keys to leave. The keys now clutched in my hand. I couldn't remember how they'd gotten there.

When we reached the door, I panicked and jabbed him in the ribs hard with my elbow. I'm sure it hurt some, but it wasn't what caused him to let me go. It was simply shock that I still had enough fire left to in any way seek to go against his wishes.

I moved away from him, but he latched onto my arm with one hand. I didn't hesitate. The keys were in my other hand, and I drove them into his skin. I expected him to cry out, but he didn't. Instead, he let go of me and cradled his hand like a wounded animal.

I felt the smallest amount of pity well up inside me and an almost compulsive urge to bandage him up, despite the fact that I hadn't drawn blood.

He gave me a look of shocked betrayal as if he had any right to it after everything. I was the one that was being betrayed. I was the one being thrown out without explanation. I turned and ran down the hallway.

It did remind me of a castle. The stonework, the extreme ornateness, the woven tapestries on the walls. I ran to the end of the hallway until I came to an open door. To call it a living room or den would have been to understate it. It was more of a home movie theater. A giant screen played CNN on one end of the room.

I stopped to watch for a minute, wondering if I was old news or if they would mention me. I wondered if they would flash my picture across the screen, back when I'd been another person. They didn't. My momentary distraction allowed him to catch up to me.

Strong arms wrapped around me like a vice, and for one insane moment I sagged back against him, soaking up the feeling of being in his embrace, even if it wasn't really an embrace. I could feel his hot breath on my ear as he bent down.

"Please don't make me leave. Whatever I did wrong I won't do it again. Just don't throw me out."

I know how this sounded, how completely pathetic, but I couldn't make my mouth not form the words. I think there was something left of me that knew this was all wrong and that I should take the opportunity for freedom that he handed me, but I didn't want that choice anymore.

He continued to hold me, everything pausing, the universe just stopping while he decided to keep me or make me go.

"Please . . . " I whispered.

He turned me to face him, his eyes locking with mine. And I couldn't read him. After months of his eyes and his body being my only signs of anything, I couldn't read him. He shoved me away onto the couch and left the room.

I sat there, numb, the keys and my freedom finally in my hands. I was afraid of him again. Actually afraid. I hadn't been actually afraid in months. Obedience had always brought reward. I learned my lessons from the cell and never repeated the mistakes.

One would think that in itself would set up a constant fear, but it didn't. After the day he'd made absolutely plain that all he expected was effort, after he proved that time and time again over months, I came to trust him more than I'd ever trusted anyone. Because even if he was a monster, he followed his own rules. And he was my monster.

He was stable in his way, dependable, predictable, and in complete control. But as I sat on the couch on the verge of a panic attack, I knew this wasn't the case any longer. He was finally behaving in the manner in which one expects a psychotic to behave, and that was truly frightening.

In this state it wouldn't take much for him to kill me, and I wasn't so far gone I would rather die than be free. Was I?

I laughed, a hollow little sound against the droning backdrop of CNN. What kind of a complete mental case has to weigh whether they would rather die or be free? Die or be a slave? Yes, that's logical. Die or be free, no.

Still I didn't move. I wondered if I was in shock. It was as if I was just beginning to realize the danger I was in.

That wasn't true.

I'd realized early on, but he'd made me forget. I'd forgotten because I'd fallen into that fathomless gaze of his and the way he made me feel everything so strongly.

He returned a few minutes later, and I tensed. He stood in the doorway, a red leather book in his hands. My journal. I didn't want to read that now. I'd just kept writing straight through without going back to reread.

In the beginning it had been a way to salvage sanity after a fashion, or else a way to document so someday when I was free I could remember all he'd done to me and make him pay. Now I couldn't go back and read it all. I wanted to keep moving forward, writing new diary entries, never looking back to what had gone on before.

He watched me. He was so conflicted I could feel it rolling off him. It was as if he didn't want to let me go but for some reason was almost compelled to do so. Was he sorry?

No, don't be sorry.

Why wouldn't he just talk to me now? If he was letting me go anyway, what purpose did these mind games serve?

Finally, he tossed the journal at me and sat in a nearby chair. Was this why he was throwing me away? Had I written something between these pages that was so unforgivable that rather than keep me in the bad cell, he'd throw me away completely? I held the soft, thick leather book in my hands and opened it.

But it wasn't my journal. It was his.

Nine

August 26th:

Today I found something beautiful and decided to break it. I wanted to see it shatter in my hand and crumble at my feet. Her name is Emily Vargas. She's bright and educated and stunning. Articulate. She'll want someone to talk to her.

I was at a convention in Nashville, one of those boring meetings where we judge the health of the company and all the stockholders bitch and whine. I really couldn't give two shits about the business, but it was my father's. I'm a fucking household name but no one knows my face, which is fine by me. I'd rather have my privacy.

Even the servants are only here once a week. They already know I'm idiosyncratic. I'm a hermit, so even as the plan was forming, I knew I could get away with it. I hate being around so many people because I have to have an interpreter like some sort of foreign person. I generally just sit in these meetings like a statue, waiting for them to be over with.

Walter does all the talking. In fact, most people believe he owns the company because he's always the one speaking for it. Most of them don't know about my handicap. I think some of the people in the meetings think I'm his bodyguard. If I was some pale scrawny kid I'm not sure how exactly we would explain my presence.

Whatever explanations would have to be done, Walter would have to do them. He's about the only person I trust not to screw me over and to keep my secrets; though my new secret is too sensitive even for him.

After the meeting was over, I wandered the hotel and sat at the bar. A woman came up and started speaking to me. She was attractive in her way, legs that ran on for a few miles at least, and cleavage I wanted to bury my face in. She smiled. I smiled. And that was about as far as the interaction could go.

"Hi, what's your name? I'm Veronica."

God, even her name dripped sex. Here was the moment. I used to just smile pathetically. Instead, I turned back to the bar.

The bartender knew me and knew what I liked, so I found a whiskey straight sitting in front of me. I threw the shot back and slammed it down on the counter. The barkeep filled it again. I knew I'd be happiest if he just kept them coming.

"God, you are such an asshole!" she said, and then she flounced off, her ass swaying delectably as she retreated. That's when I had the fantasy I always have. I'd chase her, grab her and slam her against the wall, and just fucking take her. Forget all this social bullshit. And it *is* bullshit when you can't participate.

Then I saw her, Emily. She came up to the bar. "Sam, can I get a martini?"

The bartender smiled and made her drink. She put a stack of brochures next to her, and when she looked away for a moment, I took one and slipped it into my jacket. The brochure contained her tour schedule. She drank her martini and never spoke to me.

I didn't know if I was glad about that or not. I'm not sure why she should have spoken to me. I could have been some stalker fan, and it was obvious she just needed space.

For the next twenty minutes, I listened to her lyrical voice as she flirted with the bartender, and he bantered back. It was a sexual dance that was socially acceptable to perform out in the open, the modern repressed equivalent of a Roman orgy.

When she left, I studied the brochure. I think I just snapped, but I've decided to take her. I'm so fucking tired of being alone, of paying whores or seeking out women who know sign language. In the end, they all feel sorry for me, even the whores. I've got all this money, and it doesn't mean a goddamned thing because I can't carry on a relationship with anyone without them treating me like I'm slow because of my inability to speak.

I'd rather have fear than pity.

I felt numb. I could vaguely remember that bar and the bartender. I *had* thought the man beside me might be a stalker fan, or more likely someone whose wife had left him and for whatever reason he blamed me for it.

Sometimes women in less than stellar relationships were moved by something in one of my books, developed self-esteem, and left their boyfriends or husbands or whatever. Often I got blamed for it.

I looked at him, wanting to say something. Maybe he didn't know as much about me as he thought, because surely he would have communicated with me if he did. I knew sign language because of my sister.

Of course, I could understand why he might not know that. When Katie died, mom and dad were so upset that after a few months they just erased her. Like she didn't exist. It was too hard on them.

I thought it was cruel at the time, but thinking about her just hurt too much. I considered telling him, but he was pointing at the book and the pages he'd dog-eared. The ones that held all the explanations I'd waited months for and finally had stopped believing I would get.

I wasn't sure sign language would help me now anyway because I *did* feel sorry for him. Maybe it would get me killed. He'd been in charge for so long, and now that he was showing vulnerability, surely his self-control wouldn't hold out. The edges of it seemed frayed already. Things were unraveling. So instead I went back to the journal and flipped to the next dog-eared page.

January 30th:

I know I'm fucking crazy. I've left Walter to run things for awhile. I'm never home. I've been following her tour schedule.

I understand there's something wrong with this. And I know what's wrong with it isn't so much that I'm doing it, as that I don't care it's wrong.

When you're a part of society there are certain behaviors that aren't okay. If you do these behaviors and then feel nothing, that's worse. But I've been trying to determine when I've ever been a part of society.

Even before I had a house built on what feels like the edge of the known universe, even when I mingled, I wasn't a part. I was always on the outside looking in. There was one small group of people who I could speak with through sign language, rather than just looking at them dumbly.

And now I'm fucking feeling sorry for myself. Or maybe I'm justifying. No, because I intellectually know it's wrong. I'm not an idiot. I had the best schooling that could be bought. I just don't care. And I know I'll get away with it.

During my time at home, I've converted some rooms for use when I get her. I've sound-proofed them because I'm not sure how much she'll scream. The servants are rarely there anyway, but just to be on the safe side. I set the rooms up to look like labs, except the room with the monitors. That seems normal. And I've got the doors labeled as such.

The staff knows I used to work on product research, and they'll think it's a good sign I'm starting it again. I hear them talk amongst themselves. Sometimes I catch snippets about how I don't go out much anymore and don't do anything. Well, what the fuck is there to do?

As soon as the electrical people get the security system in place for the rooms, I can start getting rid of all the lab stuff and moving in what needs to go in. Except one room I'll keep bare.

That's probably the best way. I thought about using drugs to make her comply, but that leaves more of a potential paper trail. And something could go wrong, some unforeseen side effect or allergic reaction, and then I'm left with either letting her die or risk getting caught. Plus having a druggie on my hands isn't overly appealing.

Although I have no moral problem with the course I've chosen, I don't believe I would be so cavalier about taking a life. I'm just not an overly violent person, except for the occasional sexual fantasy. I don't want to physically harm her; I just want her.

I suppose I could always do one of those pathetic attempts at a relationship again. But then we're back to me being pitied. For once I want a goddamned woman to know I'm not helpless just because I can't talk to her. I really don't think I'll have to hurt her, though. I know her weakness.

I've never seen anyone drink up social interaction in quite the starved way she does. If I deprive her of everything, she'll comply.

I watch her at these conferences she does, careful to keep to the shadows so she doesn't notice me and realize that one face is always there amidst the ever-changing sea of them. She flits around, and one can see where the term *social butterfly* comes from. She has the most musical laugh, and once or twice I almost felt guilty.

But then I close my eyes, and I see her naked beneath me, knowing that for once in my fucking life, I have absolute power with a woman. Someone who can't reject me and wouldn't know how to pity me, and the twinge is gone again.

I couldn't stop the tears tracking down my face at how casual he was about the whole thing. How he talked about breaking me like one might mention what they were having for dinner. The extreme arrogance, the lack of remorse.

I looked up again to see if now that his secret was out, he felt anything at all. All I could see was the coldness and the new restlessness that came with today. The day he was releasing me. I knew he wouldn't allow me to stay because he'd let me too far into his world now.

I still didn't know why he was doing it, but if he was letting me see the man behind the curtain, it was because he was finished with me for good.

May 3rd:

It's only a couple of weeks til she'll be in Atlanta again. I can't believe I'm really going to do this. For a few months I think I believed I wasn't going to. It was just a fantasy, like the others. I was just making it more real.

But I've spent an outrageous sum on her; by God I'm taking her. I know there is extreme hubris in taking her in her hometown, but it's the most logical for me because it's the closest to where we're going. The shorter the distance I have to transport her, the better.

I've been researching various drugs and have found one that will keep her out about four hours. The drive home, barring any problems, is only two. With my luck I'll hit traffic, though. I don't want her to wake tied up in the car. It completely ruins the effect and gives her at least a small chance of escape.

I want her to know from the beginning there is no chance of escape. Although once I move her to the luxury suite, I fully expect her to lash out somehow. It'll be best, I think, to get the rebellion out of the way early and let her see the pointlessness of her actions.

I haven't seen her since March. Instead, I've been looking into her background, learning what I can. I want her suite to have everything she likes.

On the one hand, I want to break her so completely she'll do anything I want without question. But on the other, I want her to choose me. I want her grateful and willing. I want control, but I don't want her screaming when I fuck her.

I know the world would class me a monster, but control is what turns me on, not a woman screaming or begging me not to rape them. I don't mind a little fear, I just want her to choose. If she doesn't choose me, I'll just leave her in the cell until she changes her mind. I've waited a long goddamned time for this. If she thinks she can outlast my patience, she's insane.

May 15th:

It couldn't have gone more perfectly. When she started to feel unsteady, I helped her outside. I don't think she even saw me. Then she collapsed in my arms. I had her in the car before anyone noticed she'd left. I didn't stop to secure her for a good ten minutes until I'd gotten off the main drag.

Then I pulled off on a deserted exit. I tied her hands and feet, blindfolded her, then laid her in the backseat and covered her with a blanket. I knew it was safer to put her in the trunk, but dying of carbon monoxide poisoning was a possibility, especially with drugs already running through her veins.

I had her in the cell before she woke and decided not to be in the room with her to start with, but to just watch her on the monitor. I was a bit concerned when she didn't wake exactly when she was supposed to. It took me awhile to realize she *was* awake. She just wasn't screaming or struggling.

She was smart, saving her energy, waiting for her one moment of escape, possibly retracing her steps and trying to remember what had brought her to me. I hadn't planned to touch her the first day, and I know I'll have to be more disciplined or else I'm going to end up having to hurt her.

If I don't want to hurt her, I have to do better. I have to make myself do better. But I can't completely regret it. I sat on the ground beside her, and I reached out and stroked the smoothness of her cheek. I've never felt skin so soft.

I know she was terrified. She probably thought I'd hurt her, and suddenly that bit of caring came through because it was an actual person. I'd thought of her for months as a piece of property I was acquiring, but I couldn't deny the warmth of her ragged breath, or the softness of her cheek, or the way she was already leaning into me, even if she didn't realize it.

I managed finally to pull my hand away and fed her a bite of the soup. I was surprised she hadn't started reacting yet. I found my hand reaching out to cup her breast, and she jerked away. It made me angry. Not so much that she pulled away but that I'd expected anything else. I started to leave, and her voice stopped me. Soft, desperate begging that made my pants tighten.

I returned and decided I would test her to see how far she could be pushed to eat. I knew she was still a little drugged, hungry, tired, scared. I could test her now and then wait a week like I'd planned.

By the end of the bowl of soup she was arching into my hand, letting out soft little moans that I'm pretty sure she didn't know she was making. I had the idea I could have her right then. Fuck the plan, just move her to the luxury suite, shower her with everything. But it wasn't what I wanted now.

Having her so afraid, so willing to please me if I'd feed her . . . I can't deny the effect it had on me. It's going to be a difficult seven days. I'm willing to admit what I want. I don't just want her. I don't even just want her not to pity me. I want her fear, desperation, complete and total obedience. And I am willing to wait for it.

She asked me why I was doing this to her, and for once I was glad I couldn't speak. My silence will help mold her, my hands will become my voice, and eventually she won't know the difference and won't care. Breaking her will be the best thing I've ever done.

May 18th:

She acted out much like I expected, throwing her soup like a child. I believe she still thought I was planning to kill her and wanted me to lose control and do it quickly. It's the only explanation I can think of for the behavior.

I've scoured every behavioral psych book I could get my hands on for months. Although I'm quite sure the authors didn't intend for it to be used this way.

At first I studied it to try to understand her better, since she'd gotten her degree in psychology. Then I decided to use it to condition her because there's nothing quite so insidious as torturing someone in a way so they know exactly what you're doing but know they can't escape it.

No, I'm not really physically violent, but I guess I *am* sadistic. I cleaned up the mess she made and then left her. She ruined her food; she isn't getting more. Once she learns the tantrums are useless and don't affect me, she'll stop doing it.

It was strange and unsettling, seeing these events through his eyes. It was even weirder to see a confirmation that we'd understood one another from the beginning. I hadn't suspected he was mute, of course. I should have, probably, but he was so calculating with everything else he did, why would I assume a handicap of some sort? Especially one so rare?

Muteness often comes with deafness, as with my sister. And he clearly wasn't deaf. He'd turned at the sound of my voice many times. He hadn't just been reading my lips.

Aside from that, I'd been right about everything, and he'd been right about me. Communicating without words had taken us both to a place where we had to just instinctively *get* each other. I swiped at another tear as it trailed down my cheek and looked up at him.

"Please don't make me go," I said. I'd just put the journal down so I could sign as I spoke.

His eyes widened. He genuinely hadn't known I could sign. What are the odds right? Life is strange, but there it is. I should have guessed the mute thing at least considering my family history.

Why hadn't that been one of my questions on the few days I'd been brave enough to ask them? In hindsight, it was probably best I didn't think of it.

We'd both existed in a world where people spoke with their hands, and yet neither of us had suspected the other.

I'd come to see him as omnipotent and all-knowing. In my mind he knew every detail of my life, but he wouldn't be able to get every detail practically. I realized most of them he'd probably gotten from going to my seminars. I talked a lot about my personal life at the conferences. Probably more than I should have. But I'd never talked about my sister.

He stared at me for a long while before he finally signed back.

Read.

I skipped to the next dog-eared section. I thought if I did what he said without fighting him, maybe he'd realize I was worth keeping.

That thought unhinged me. The only thing keeping me from having a complete meltdown was the idea that he was letting me go because he was trying to do the right thing. So I kept reading.

June 16th:

As thrilling as it was to see her submit, to give me her body like a wrapped-up present, I knew it wasn't real. Not yet. She still wanted out. Once she saw the rooms I'd given her, she knew what she was.

When you give someone your body in exchange for anything, you're a whore, and nothing drives that home like ridiculous levels of luxury. As I watched her on the monitor last night I could see the wheels in her head turning as she planned to attack me, the way she studied objects in her rooms that she'd never looked at so closely before.

The attempt was weak. It's not that she didn't try, she just never had a chance since I could see her waiting by the door with her weapons before I came into the room. The moment it all backfired, she was once again the scared little rabbit I'd first taken, cowering away from me.

I'm not sure I was able to keep off my face how much it affected me now to see her like that. I love the submission, but the fear drives me as well. I stretched my hand toward her and was surprised by how fast she took it. The resignation and acceptance in her eyes. And I knew I'd only have to put her back in the cell once more, and after that she'd be mine forever.

I took her outside and showed her around the grounds, then figured I'd let her try to run. I'm sure if I were an average, merely frustrated man, that by this point her tears would affect me in a way besides making me hard. The helpless obedience would turn my stomach or make me feel the twinges of guilt, and yet it doesn't. Whatever little feeling from before must have been leftover from what I'd always been taught was right and wrong.

I'm sure if I had a voice, I would still have done it. I didn't realize that until I saw her walking away from me, knowing she couldn't get far. She was prey, and it brought out a predatory instinct I'd suppressed for far too long.

When she'd gotten far enough away, I got up and began to chase her. It was as if an invisible thread tied us together because I think she sensed me behind her long before she could have heard me running. She started to run, and it felt like a game to me. To her it was survival and escape, but to me it was just fun.

Then when I knew she could hear me, she tensed, and only moments before I could have reached her and tackled her to the ground, she stopped and turned to me, her hands held out in surrender. If I have this dark need to have complete power over her, she has an equal almost pathological need to give it to me.

I would never have expected her to react like that. Fear of pain drives her in such an extreme way that she won't fight. In some ways her fear of pain seems greater than her fear of anything else, even death. Because I hadn't hurt her yet, she already trusted that if she obeys me, I won't start. I'm not about to disabuse her of that notion.

I've been working to communicate it from the beginning. She's safe if she obeys me. I just didn't expect such dramatic obedience in a moment when freedom at least felt real and possible, if for no other reason than she was outside the house in the open air.

I wanted to throw her down and fuck her right there in the grass, but I've been training her to see fucking as a reward, and so to do that would erase everything I've done so far. I gritted my teeth and turned to lead her back to the house. I've already decided it will be two weeks this time, and I'm not sure how I'm going to manage to abstain from touching her.

June 30th:

I considered making her wait until July 4th to get back to the nice rooms. I was tempted. I'm probably a bit too amused with irony. Move her back there on the day of independence. I'm sure she equates that room with freedom at this point.

While she was locked up this last time, I realized I do want to hurt her. I just don't want to hurt her out of anger. And I want her to want me to hurt her. I had a lot of time to think about all this while I was waiting. I ended up getting another room outfitted as a dungeon.

I hadn't thought I would go this route, but the more I fantasize about her, the more I see myself whipping her. And really, what else was I going to do for the two weeks of torturous waiting? A project was what I needed.

I guess it started out wanting to punish her. I wouldn't give her tampons or pads, so she ended up going about the cell naked, and who could blame her? I suppose bleeding on herself naked was better if I wasn't going to give her anything to stop her from making a mess. But I kept seeing her body on the screen, and I wanted to punish her because I had to wait. I couldn't take her without fucking up all my progress.

One day she talked to me. She got pretty panicked over the idea that she might get pregnant and I'd kill her. I have no idea why she'd think that, but she's a smart girl and figured out just by my facial expressions that I can't have kids. Just never wanted them, and the vasectomy made the problem go away. All she knows, of course, is that I'm sterile, and she doesn't have to fear that.

She asked me to talk to her again, said she'd do anything I wanted if I would. It pissed me off. I believed she would have. But I need her to submit knowing I might never speak to her. Because I can't. I'm not here to please her; she's here to please me. Even if I could speak, I don't think I would. There are no compromises here.

She will obey or she will be punished. If I'm extreme enough in the beginning with the deprivation, her fear will drive her to please me, and I won't have to worry about correcting bad behavior later or traumatizing her worse than is absolutely necessary.

As I started to leave that day, she begged me to take her out of there and not leave her alone. I jerked off for the next week to the memory of the desperation in her voice and the way her lip quivered when she spoke to me.

Then, of course, once she stopped bleeding, she still went around naked. By this time she was trying to tempt me, and I was glad she had another week left in there. I wanted to get rid of all the variations of rebellion that she had.

One day she got so brazen as to lie on the floor and masturbate, knowing I was watching. I jerked off watching her on the monitor and managed to finish before she did so I could catch her and still be in control of myself. Because she *did* have an effect, but that doesn't matter. She will not lead me by my dick like other women have. She's mine. She'll learn it and she won't forget it.

I stared her down until she stopped and then left the room. It was time for the book. I wanted her to understand I was her master, and I couldn't think of any way to convey this information. If I left her a note, she'd know of my handicap or at least suspect it. So I figured I'd be as fucking creepy about it as possible.

During her imprisonment, while working on the dungeon, I'd started highlighting the word *master* every time it appeared in an erotic novel from her room. I watched, fascinated as she walked around the book several times before finally picking it up. She thought it was a trick. I could see on the monitors how afraid she was of making the wrong choice, not knowing what I wanted from her.

She really is more than I ever could have hoped for. When I first decided to take her, it was because she was just so goddamned beautiful. And now I know she is completely surprising.

Even studying conditioning methods, I don't think I could have hoped for a better slave. When I came back into the cell, I waited. I was a bit disappointed at first when she didn't address me. I turned to leave, and that's when she said it.

"Master, please."

Those words, coming out of her mouth. That was her ticket out, lesson over. I'd decided to fuck her ass, and if she submitted to that without a fuss, I'd move her back to the suite.

I was as careful as possible. I didn't want to rip her. I just knew this was possibly the most vulnerable I could make her, even after everything else, and if she would give this to me she was completely mine.

It was better than I'd thought it would be, and afterward I just held her. I needed her to know that if she obeyed, I would touch her, I'd let her come, I'd hold her. All she had to do was give me her will completely and accept her position. There is no escape and she knows that now. She can die in the cell or she can submit.

I stopped reading. There was more, but I couldn't read anymore, not from that day.

I couldn't stand to read his reaction to whipping me, his arousal at my fear and helplessness. I skimmed through the rest of the dog-eared pages looking for one thing, why he was letting me go.

But it wasn't there. Even the last entry had only talked about our most recent time together. There was no indication he was tired of me, nor was there any hint he was sorry. I looked up then. I half expected him to insist I keep reading, but I didn't want to see anymore. I'd seen enough.

"Are you sorry you did this to me?"

He shrugged.

"Why are you letting me go? *Are* you letting me go?"

Yes. You're free to go. I'm releasing you because I'm finished with you.

Just like that. He was finished with me. He'd taken me and considered me a toy, property, and now like any toy the owner was bored with, I was being thrown in the trash.

I wanted to fall to my knees and beg him not to do it, but the bored expression in his eyes told me it would do no good. He put the keys back in my hand.

The garage door is open, and if you press the button you'll see which car it is. The headlights will flash. You should be able to find your way easily enough.

"This doesn't make any sense. Yeah, maybe you're done with me, but why just let me go with something that can be tied to you? Aren't you concerned I'll go to the police?"

Maybe I shouldn't have said that. After all, bringing up the police could buy me a hole in the ground instead of my freedom.

He shrugged again. *I don't care one way or the other. Go take back your life, Emily.*

It took him longer to spell out my name, a word that had become so disconnected from my being. I couldn't believe I didn't want to go. I'd thought there would be something in the journal that would explain something, but every explanation was one I'd expected.

"Did I not please you? Did I do something wrong?"

I knew even as I said the words that a normal person would take their freedom and not ask questions, but I'd been with him so long I'd come to depend on him. He'd offered me a kind of security I'd never experienced, even if it was somewhat warped in its nature.

You pleased me. You did nothing wrong. You exceeded my expectations. But now you need to leave.

"Can I take a few things?" Mementos. How fucked up was that? I wanted reminders of my imprisonment.

He nodded.

I didn't take much. A few Middle Eastern CD's—the drumbeats would calm me—some candles, a few favorite outfits, and my journal, the pages all written in. Full. It was a strange sort of poetry.

I had always thought when I got to the end of the journal that he would buy me a new one, not release me.

I didn't think it was anything more than coincidence that the two events coincided, but it was as if I'd written a book, and I'd run out of space, so I had run out of captivity as well. I took the things out to the garage and loaded them into the car.

I don't know why I didn't try to beg more. I guess there was a part of me that knew I really couldn't stay. He was giving me my life back and to refuse that gift was unthinkable.

I'd obeyed him so very long now that to receive an order, the instinct was to obey, no matter how much I didn't want to. Not out of fear of punishment, but out of a desire to please him and gain and keep his favor.

Of all the things he'd wanted from me, this was the hardest to obey. I really had lost my mind. No sane person would be so horrified by the idea of freedom. But surely when I saw my family and friends again, things would be different, and I could put all of this behind me.

TEN

He didn't have to forcibly remove me from the house because I knew he would and having a breakdown at this point wasn't going to help. I had belonged to him, and now he was showing me how absolute that was by disposing of me like any other piece of property that had become of little interest.

The car he'd given me was a silver Mercedes, and truly it was a gift because what was the likelihood I'd bring it back? I dumped everything but the CDs into the trunk on top of a car emergency kit. A small shovel clattered when the journal hit it.

It took forever to get out of the driveway. It really did seem to go on forever. Part of me wondered if it was all an elaborate test to make me come back, but then I'd seen the absoluteness in his eyes, and there was no reason to show me my helplessness. I knew it; I'd taken it into the deepest part of my being, and I'd accepted it. No further object lessons were needed.

The car didn't have a global positioning system, something I found odd. I ripped the *this journal belongs to* page out of the red leather book and started writing reverse directions, like a trail of bread crumbs, recording where I went so I wouldn't get lost.

After a couple of lucky and arbitrary turns, I came to a busier road. At least I'd found civilization again and could ask for help if I needed it. Though I wasn't sure I wanted to deal with the possibility of being recognized as *that self-help guru that had gone missing.* So I kept going until I found the interstate.

When I finally got there, I discovered I was about thirty miles from home. Not starting from the interstate but including the bumble where I'd been. I'd assumed I was thousands of miles away from home in some remote location. To learn I'd been just thirty miles away from my house the whole damn time made me crave the freedom I'd thought I'd given up.

I'd been listening to one of the Middle Eastern CDs. The music hadn't calmed me so much as made me want to turn the car around, but I didn't. There was some tiny screaming sliver of me that still wanted to be free. Finally, I couldn't stand the drums any longer.

I took the disc out but resisted the urge to break it, some part of my mind still convinced I might want to listen to it again someday in the future when the wounds weren't as fresh. I turned on the radio and remembered it was Halloween.

I expected the date to make me feel giddy. Instead, driving through suburbia I found myself disconcerted by all the sensory input. The decorations. The kids running around in costumes at afternoon parties. I found myself bizarrely frightened of the imaginary creatures which within hours would be going bump in the night.

I couldn't go to my house first. It was a rental, and somehow I doubted anyone would have kept up the rent for the almost six months I'd been missing. As I drove down the Magnolia-lined street my parents lived on, the radio ceased being background noise.

"A memorial service was held yesterday for self-help guru, Emily Vargas, as police still have found no leads to her mysterious disappearance. When contacted for comment, the family expressed a need for closure and would offer no more . . . "

I nearly swerved off the road. They'd erased me. Just like my sister. What kind of family waits only six months before burying an empty box to just get on with it?

Surely most would wait a year, maybe even two. I understood how hard it had to be considering losing Katie like they had, but it felt like rejection, as if I had no place left in the world to go to.

I drove past the house and went to the cemetery. I searched the family plots until I found mine. It was surreal and more upsetting than I expected it to be, and I couldn't help but feel completely betrayed by my family for acting so selfishly, for not thinking about how this might make me feel after what I'd experienced. How did they expect to explain it to me if I was ever found?

There were still-blooming flowers all around the grave, the dirt fresh and piled high. Some crazy part of me wanted to dig the coffin out, if in fact there was one. If there wasn't, I couldn't imagine what it was they'd seen fit to bury.

I tried to picture my family and friends wearing black, sobbing over my supposed death based on the fact that my parents couldn't carry the torch just a little bit longer, and I was disgusted.

I stared at the gravestone. *Emily Vargas: devoted friend, loving daughter, inspiring leader.* My death was marked as the day before, the day of the funeral.

Goddammit!

I kicked at and scattered the pile of dirt. What the hell gave them the right to just kill me off? It was inconvenient for me to exist and be missing?

I don't know if it was what they'd done, or if it was because of the inability to act out for so long, but the rage flipped in me like a switch. It was something I'd forgotten I had. I didn't know I could feel anger like that; I hadn't felt it in so long.

I threw flowers and arrangements as far as I could and fell to my knees digging into the dirt, clawing at it, as if clawing to get inside. It was the reverse of being buried alive. Maybe I should be in there and not out here under the open sky with the birds chirping and everything so innocent and bright.

I'd once seen a movie about someone buried alive that somehow escaped their coffin and clawed to the surface. They were buried in a pine box, but even so, one would think the weight of the dirt would make escape impossible. If the work of digging to a box was this difficult, I couldn't imagine the reality of digging out of one.

Even though my progress was insignificant, I continued to dig. I didn't care how impossible it was, I had to get in there. I remembered the emergency kit and retrieved the shovel from the trunk of the car, thankful for a master who was compulsively prepared for any traveling contingency.

As I continued to dig with the small shovel, I worried the police would show up. Surely they kept a closer eye on cemeteries on Halloween. But it was early afternoon, and the troublemakers wouldn't be out until after the sun had gone down. I thought about kids out making mischief stumbling upon my dug-out grave and having a ghost story to pass around.

I finally got to the coffin. I had the momentary fear I would open it and see my body in there, that I really was gone and somehow didn't know it yet. But when I opened the lid there was no body, only things of mine. Old ballet shoes, journals, photographs. Things that became me in the absence of a body to put in the earth.

Now, out in the fresh air, looking at what was meant as evidence of my passing, I couldn't let myself think the word *master.* But I had nothing else to call him, except *the monster who had taken me.* In the end the most monstrous thing he did was let me go. Especially in light of the fact that everyone else had let me go, too.

I wanted to get in the car and go back to him, throw myself on his mercy and hope that at least one person in the world still wanted me. But I knew I wouldn't. He'd broken me, but he'd been so strangely gentle about it that somehow I was still me inside.

I wasn't a shell, a hollowed-out zombie of a human being, though at this moment, with graveyard dirt covering me virtually head to toe, I looked like it. For whatever reason, he wanted me to be free, and I'd been trained to obey. I could keep going if I thought of it as obedience.

I gathered my stuff from the coffin and took it to the car. I'd found a twenty-dollar bill in my pocket, so I stopped at a drive-through for some food. My master must have slipped money into the jeans before he'd tossed them to me that morning.

Thinking of how well he took care of me ripped me apart inside, and I had to hold back the floodgates because I was in public. The girl at the drive through looked at me oddly as I paid for my cheeseburger meal.

"I'm a zombie," I said dully. I almost laughed at my own joke.

The light bulb went off over her head as she looked down at her clothes and remembered it was Halloween. She was about seventeen with blonde hair that had pink streaks in it and going for a slutty Punky Brewster effect with her clothing. Probably she was passing it off as a costume because she didn't have the nerve to wear it any other day.

"Oh, right. Clever," she said. "The dirt makeup looks real."

I smiled, biting back the urge to say it *was* real dirt. I ate in the parking lot, then started the car again. I needed to get cleaned up, but I knew I didn't have a house to go to except for my parents' place, and I wasn't ready to see them just yet.

I hadn't been in the house for long when I'd been taken, and still had my storage unit. It had held all the things in my house before they went into my house, and I'd paid a year in advance because you never know when you might need a storage facility.

I hadn't been sure the new place would work out. I blame my mother for this insane level of over-planning. I have no other excuses.

My storage unit, like all of them at the ultra-modern facility, worked by a combination keypad, and I was the only one who knew the code.

My fingers trembled as I punched it in, then drove the car into it like a garage and turned off the ignition. I'd known from the moment I got out the door I wouldn't call the police. I would never tell them anything that had happened, or lead them down the winding roads to the house that had been my prison.

I sat in the car, going through the things that had been buried in the coffin, reading the journals, looking at who I'd been, or who they'd simplified me down to in order to fit me into a box, and it struck me how much they didn't really know anything about me. Whether it was by my own omissions or their lack of observation I would never know.

My house was fifteen miles away from that of my parents, and it was that way because it was the opposite end of town, as far as I could get and still be in the same place. The storage facility was only five miles from their house, which made walking much easier.

Once the car was taken care of and I was walking down the streets through the residential neighborhood, the enormity of my situation hit me.

Kids were running down the streets beside me all dressed up like pumpkins and pirates and ghosts, shrieking and laughing, their candy pails swinging from their arms as exhausted parents tried to keep up with them.

It was too much. Everything was too loud. Even the drive-through had been difficult. To have a human being speak to me. To have any set of eyes on me but his . . . it was unnerving, an invasion. It made me feel naked and exposed.

Over months of being with him, my prison had become my sanctuary, and now that I was free, the world was my prison. There was nowhere left to run.

No one paid much attention to me as I walked. I'm sure part of it was that the sun was setting behind the trees, and the stark afternoon brightness of a few hours before was long gone. I wasn't recognizable as Emily. Anyone who saw me didn't look horrified or shocked. I was just wearing a costume like everybody else.

It was full dark when I reached my parents' house. Their porch was lit with the typical Halloween array, a giant lit-up pumpkin, bats hanging from the porch, a bloody scarecrow lying over a bale of hay in the front yard.

They really had just erased me, had some kind of psychotic fit that allowed them to shut that door and open another one. To lay me to rest and the next day give out candy to neighborhood kids and do the normal

Halloween things without it necessary to give me a second thought. It was obscene.

I'd seen them when Katie had died. I knew it was because the only way they could survive was to behave like this. Still. To not openly grieve and mourn, to instead hide and bury and erase. It wasn't the way normal human beings behaved toward those they were supposed to love. Even if those they loved were only a memory now.

When I knocked, my mother shouted from behind the door, "Ted, get that!"

I heard something fall and break, a stream of curses, and then the door flew open. My mother's irritation turned to shock.

"Ted!" she screamed, as if her shouts could protect her from the daughter who wouldn't die and be gone forever like a good little girl.

My father came to stand behind her in the doorway, "Donna, what is it?" His face went pale when he saw me, looking morbidly as if I'd crawled out of my grave.

I wanted to say it served them right for burying someone who wasn't dead in the first place, but it wasn't my dad's fault, not really. He just went along with whatever my mother said to do.

Finally, I found my voice. "Mom . . . "

"You're not real," she said. It wasn't said like someone who actually missed their daughter and was thrilled to have her home. It was said as if my appearance on her doorstep screwed up her 12-step plan to deny I'd ever existed. Such was the way of the Vargas clan.

Perhaps I should have gone somewhere else. But it was a perverse revenge, and I was unwilling to play this morbid scene out with anyone who didn't deserve it.

"I'm real, mom."

"But we didn't bury you. You're covered in dirt."

My father stood behind my mom, his hands on her shoulders, steadying her as if he controlled anything in that house.

"No, you didn't bury me. Did you not think that maybe I wasn't dead, or was that not convenient for you?"

I understood they must have suffered when they'd thought they'd lost me. The sleepless nights, the fear for my safety. But it didn't change the fact that they'd buried me to make their lives easier, so they could go on when I hadn't had that luxury.

Then the tears started. Not mine. I was fairly certain I didn't have tears left to cry. I'd used up my lifetime supply, and from now on my sobs would be verbal rather than wet. No, it was my mother crying. I was hurting her feelings.

"How could you say such a vile thing to me? We were worried sick. Where were you? What happened to you?"

Now it was time to accuse me. I'd not yet been invited into the house. I was still standing on the porch next to a giant plastic illuminated jack-o-lantern with a goofy grin on his face. A trail of trick-or-treaters stopped me from speaking.

"Trick-or-treat!" they caroled out, their treat bags held out like little beggars. One of the girls was dressed up like a witch. She'd managed to wipe off some of her green face make-up, and the wart was about to fall right off her nose.

My mother grabbed me by the arm and pulled me inside before giving the kids candy and sending them on their way. She shut the door and whirled on me.

She looked ridiculous wearing a pink bathrobe and slippers because Halloween was the one day of the year she could get away with being a slob. She had the bowl clutched in her hands so tightly I thought the glass would shatter and the candy would go flying onto the floor like a pinata. Her hands had gone white from gripping, and her face matched her hands. And yet . . . she was angry, not afraid.

"Where have you been?" She said it as if I'd been out playing hooky or something. Like I would disappear for months without a word on a joy ride and then come back looking like I did just for the hell of it.

I opened my mouth and then shut it again. Now that I was back, everyone would want to know. The police would want a statement, as would the media and all my friends and family. They felt they were entitled to know. I'd been gone, throwing their lives into a tailspin, and now I owed it to them to tell them, at least something. At least the barest, most TV movie-of-the-week version.

But I couldn't bring myself to do it. To be forced to tell what had happened felt like rape, another violation and another choice that wasn't free. I'd exposed every inch of my body and soul to one man for months, until force became voluntary. I wasn't doing it again just in a different form.

Besides, I thought it was reasonable to think that once you bury someone, you give up rights to hearing their story. I wasn't going to forgive them easily.

"I can't talk about it," I said. My voice quivered. I'm sure they thought it was trauma, but it was anger.

My mother nodded in understanding; my father still hadn't said a word to me. Oh he loved me, in his way. He just wasn't good at expressing it.

"I need to get cleaned up," I said. After hours of dirt caked on me, I was becoming less and less appealing.

"You can use the guest room and bathroom, and wear some of my clothes. I'll make you something to eat," my mother said.

I wished I'd brought the clothes from the Mercedes, but I didn't want any evidence that would help the police find my captor. It was irrational. I should want him locked up forever for what he'd done, but I didn't. The thought of him locked in some cage turned my stomach.

I stopped off at my mother's closet and got a T-shirt and some jeans in my size, which was six sizes ago for my mother. But like most women, she kept the hope alive that someday she'd get back into her skinny jeans.

The guest bedroom had previously been my bedroom. I wondered how long it had taken after my disappearance for them to start the erasing process? Packing my stuff up and redecorating the room.

The last time I'd been in this room had been a little more than a year ago. At that time it had remained untouched from my childhood, as if my parents expected that one day I would age backwards and they'd need it again.

There had been Barbie dolls and toys, as well as nail polish and posters of then-current rock stars, items from a room gone from childhood to teen. It had stood as some sort of unnatural shrine to keep me there, even after I'd freed myself from my cage and gone to college and then created a life of my own.

Now it was all gone. I wondered if they'd had a massive yard sale, or if it was all in storage somewhere, or up in the attic, out of sight out of mind. Now it looked like a country bed and breakfast. White wicker furniture and soft pale lavender carpet.

There was a delicate white crocheted bedspread and a border on the wall of wisteria, then the bottom half more pale lavender, stripes on white. An antique lamp and an old-fashioned alarm clock stood on the nightstand. There was not one shred of evidence I'd ever been there, as if it were my parents who had a crime to cover up.

I'd taken my shoes off at the door, so as not to track dirt into the bedroom. The bathroom had that same hollow *guest* feeling. Like the bedroom, it was warm and cozy but it looked like it belonged in a magazine, not that anyone could actually live in there. If I couldn't find a friend to stay with until I got my stuff back and figured out, then I'd be stuck staying here in this warm sterility.

There was no trace of the bathroom of my childhood. It was a hunter green with lots of houseplants and ivy wallpaper that looked like it was randomly crawling over the walls. The linoleum had been taken up and new tile put down. The shower curtain was transparent.

I stepped out of the dirty clothes and turned on the water. After the first day he'd shaved me, it had been spelled out that any stubble would send me back to the bad cell. The promise of three weeks loomed over me as threatening in my mind as a sentence to death row.

One night I had stubble. He almost took me to the cell, but I begged him to watch the video so he'd know I'd obeyed him. He must have done so because when he returned, he'd nodded as if everything were okay.

Standing in the shower now, with the water pouring over me, I could feel the stubble. It would be normal, expected even, for me to leave it alone and let it grow, like some arcane and hidden secret proof of my freedom, but I couldn't do it. Instead, I grabbed a razor and shaved, knowing I'd never let that hair grow out again even if no one ever knew about it either way, or why I did it.

After I was clean, shaven, and my hair was washed with mango-scented shampoo, I leaned my forehead against the wall and cried. Yes, I still could.

Out in the entryway I'd held it together. I'd had to keep myself from flinching when I'd heard my mother's voice grating like fingernails on a chalkboard. And for once, my father's silence had been appreciated.

I wondered if I would ever get used to hearing human speech besides my own again. I'd heard human voices on CDs I'd been given, but they were singing. Singing always seemed disconnected from reality, since aside from musicals, people don't just randomly burst into song.

I got out of the shower, dressed, and then went to sit on the foreign bed. Probably the same mattress that had always been there, but who knew? Despite being hungry, I stayed there until my mother knocked on the door.

"Honey, I've fixed you something to eat. Come on into the kitchen."

She'd shifted gears, and now she was prepared to deal with my existence again. When I got to the kitchen, I had to stop the scream from coming out of my mouth. I'm sure she thought it was the logical thing to do, that it would somehow comfort me. She couldn't have known it would never comfort me again.

"Emmie?" My childhood nickname. "Honey, I made you some chicken noodle soup. It always made you feel better before."

Before. Not now. And never again. How exactly did one explain an inexplicable phobic reaction to chicken soup?

"I'm sorry, I can't eat this," I said. It was as if his punishment followed me, and I wondered what I'd done to displease him.

Rationally, I knew my mother was just doing what made sense to her, what she'd always done. The one food Band-aid that had always worked before. Unfortunately this food was now a knife, not a bandage, and cutting on me more wouldn't make it better.

"Why the hell not?"

I knew she was trying to believe I was being difficult. She was still holding onto the diminishing hope that I hadn't been horribly tortured, that instead I'd gone off irresponsibly on a trip or had a late quarter-life crisis.

"I can't talk about it," I said, "I just can't eat that."

She started to open her mouth again, but my father stepped in, in one of those rare and miraculous instances where he doesn't let her get away with just anything.

"Donna, I think if Emmie doesn't want chicken noodle soup, she can have something else. We've got some leftover spaghetti."

"That'd be fine, Dad." I was relieved.

The last thing I needed was a shouting match with my mother because I couldn't fit either the image of someone desperately grateful for chicken noodle soup, or that of some rebellious teenager. My mother lit a cigarette and sat in front of the television.

Soup was her entire repertoire. I guess being in the cell I'd overly romanticized it. When you're someone's prisoner, the idea of mom is idealized. All neurotic and annoying behavior is swept under the rug in light of that need to just be safe.

I followed my dad into the kitchen, unwilling to deal with her. I wasn't about to explain to them about the soup. For one thing, I had no idea how to edit it down into some parent-safe version of the events. And for another, even if I could, they would suspect what had gone on, and I couldn't handle the idea that my parents might suspect, even in the most vague way, the things that had gone on between my master and myself. That was private.

My dad busied himself in the kitchen, taking the spaghetti out of the fridge and loading up a plate for me. "You want garlic bread?"

"Yeah."

I helped myself to some tea out of the fridge.

"You okay?" he asked. He didn't look at me. I could hear the catch in his voice. If he cried, there was no hope for any of us.

"I'm fine," I said. It wasn't true, and I couldn't exactly express that the largest reason it was a lie was because I was free. I didn't think he had the proper wiring to understand that one.

He just nodded. "Your mother was worried. We both were. She may be acting a little funny, but she just doesn't know how to process some things."

"I know."

And I did know. The tragedy of both my parents was that neither of them was a bad person. They had always loved me and my sister. They just couldn't always cope with things. Although I suspected that the not coping came largely from my mother's side of the camp.

When the microwave dinged, I took the plate and plowed through it like a starving woman. It was my first real food of the day. I didn't count fast food, and I hadn't had breakfast.

My father stood in the kitchen for a few minutes more, watching me. It was obvious he wanted to say something else, and I knew what it was. He wanted to know which version of reality was true. Had I been someone's prisoner, so he could be distraught? Or had I just run off, so he could be angry? But he remained stoic as ever.

With the dirt that had covered me, one might assume something at least resembling what had happened. But if I'd had a mental breakdown and run off somewhere, only to come back and discover a fresh grave with my name on it, the results would have been the same. They were better off not knowing. They'd be better off angry.

The doorbell rang again. More kids. I put the empty plate in the sink and headed for the door. I wanted to do something normal. Even if my heart wasn't in it, I wanted to participate in some inane activity like giving candy to random neighborhood kids in costumes.

My mother had been halfway to the entryway when I stopped her and took the bowl of candy from her hand and opened the door. But it wasn't cherub-faced little princesses and miniature goblins that greeted me. I had believed I'd been discreet, that no one had recognized me, but I'd been wrong.

The glass bowl shattered on the porch and the candy went flying.

A crowd of journalists had assembled on my lawn with bright lights and cameras and microphones. Some of them with little squares of paper that they were furiously jotting notes down on. Perhaps noting my state of dress, my facial expressions, whether or not I looked abused or if I'd lost or gained any weight.

I squinted out into the sea of eager faces, people for whom my trauma equaled their paycheck. I could hear camera shutters clicking, could see the video cameras trained on me, and I wondered if he would be watching the news back in his fortress. Just another piece of video surveillance. Just another way he could spy on me.

"Miss Vargas." It wasn't one voice, it was several, all bleeding together, running on a loop.

"Why didn't you go to the police?"

"Were you kidnapped? Is the perpetrator still at large?"

"Emily . . . "

"Miss Vargas, were you held against your will?"

"What happened?"

"Can we get a statement?"

"Miss Vargas . . . "

I shut the door and locked it. The nightmare had begun.

ELEVEN

I left my family to handle the media and the random people who kept popping by insisting we were the closest of friends and they needed to see how I was, when really, most of them had the most fleeting and peripheral impact on my life.

They just wanted to rubberneck. These people built up our association so they could watch with morbid fascination the undoing of one Emily Vargas.

I had no choice but to talk to the police. I'd already decided I wouldn't turn him in. The idea of the man I'd called master being locked up was more distressing to me than anything else I'd experienced.

I would have loved to have refused to talk, but then I'd be obstructing justice. *Justice.* As if anyone but me had any horse in that race. It was a crime against me, not the police, or the state, or the country. To force me to comply was just one more type of enslavement. So I did what I had to do. I lied.

I told them I never knew exactly where I was, but that one day he tied me up and blindfolded me, drove for what seemed like several hours, and then dropped me off on the side of a highway. By the time I got through the ropes and blindfold, he was long gone. I told them I'd found out, through hitchhiking, that I was in Nebraska and took rides from several people until I got home.

Of course, this was announced on the evening news along with a plea for anyone who'd picked up someone meeting my description on the route I'd described, to please call in with any additional information. A few people called.

Whether they were crank callers trying to get fifteen minutes of fame, or people who had picked up a hitch-hiker and thought it was me, it was enough to cause the investigation to grind to a halt. There just wasn't enough information to find anything.

I'd burned the clothing and shoes I was wearing, feigning naiveté and talking about how it was just too much, and I needed to get rid of the memories. No one knew about the storage facility.

The year lease was coming up, and I'd have to pay another year or switch to monthly soon. I wondered how long I was prepared to pay to shield my tormentor from punishment and if this wasn't just another way for him to hurt me.

Once the business with the police was finished, I fell into a listless pattern of television watching. A few friends came by, but I didn't have the energy or will to ask to stay with any of them. That felt too much like moving on with my life. My life had ended with him.

Everything was still too loud. Too much stimuli from too many sources. I longed for that nice, quiet room with the soft Middle Eastern drumbeats that thrummed through my body as the whip came down. To feel his weight covering me, his mouth on mine.

I'd forgotten how frantic the world was, how desperately quick everything moved, each person racing against their own clock. I was letting myself go, not taking care of my appearance.

I knew my career was over permanently. How could I ever *motivate or empower* anyone ever again? What else was left for me?

Strangely, though I didn't care about my hair or makeup and wore a grungy T-shirt and shorts most days, I continued to compulsively shave my pussy bare every time I took a shower. It was my last remaining connection to my master.

At night, my hand would drift between my legs to stroke myself off. I don't know whether I was trying to go back to him or whether I was just using an old insomnia cure, pleasure to induce sleep.

When I did sleep, he was always there. Even dreams of the bad cell most would consider nightmares held an odd sort of comfort because I knew he was watching and not far away. He'd come for me.

I'd wake around nine in the morning and then force myself to go back to sleep until I was getting up at two and three in the afternoon, all in the effort to stay unconscious as long as possible so I didn't have to face the cold reality freedom had turned out to be. Three weeks went by like this until my mother took matters into her own hands.

"I've made an appointment with Doctor Blake," she said one morning, "You know how much she helped me after your sister died."

I stared at the television, watching an afternoon rerun of a trashy talk show. I didn't take my eyes from the screen because I knew I wouldn't be able to hide my contempt.

Sure Dr. Blake had helped her, which was why she hadn't once mentioned I'd even had a sister since she died. Until just this moment.

"Did you hear me?"

"Yes, I heard you," I said.

"Well, are you going?"

"Oh, so you're asking me now?"

She sighed loudly and tapped her foot on the floor. I rolled my eyes. I didn't want more drama.

I'd been hoping to just curl up and die, but since that wasn't happening, I was going to have to do something. If Dr. Blake couldn't help, maybe she could keep me doped up. That was the next best thing.

"Sure, Mom. I'll go."

The shrink's office was exactly as I'd remembered it. It was in the city, in a high-rise building on the fifth floor. Elevator music straight out of the fifties played nonstop, the same few songs over and over.

It was like a psychotic Prozac-addled pastiche. If you weren't crazy going in, you were almost certain to be crazy coming out. I sat in one of the dark navy leather chairs and flipped through a magazine.

I'd had to convince my mother to let me drive. If I were suicidal I would have done it already. I didn't have some pressing need to swerve into oncoming traffic. I wasn't sure anyway how one could kill themselves if they were already dead.

I read the same article featured in every issue of trendy women's magazines about shocking sex secrets. Maybe I was jaded, but every one of these articles shared the same tips in just a different order. And far from being shocking, or even a little naughty, they were tame and seemed the product of a stunted sexuality rather than the type of things written by a sexually vibrant and liberated woman.

There was one other person in the room, a middle-aged balding man waiting to see the other doctor in the office. He kept muttering to himself, and when I listened closely I could hear he was counting. I had no idea what he was counting, but I knew he was going to have some kind of fit if the rug remained crooked. He'd stared at it nonstop since my arrival.

Occasionally, he'd reach out his hand as if tempted to straighten it. Then he'd pull it back quickly. I wondered if he was wearing a discreet shock collar for behavioral modification.

Before I could observe more obsessive-compulsive behavior, my name was called, and I left elevator music hell to join Doctor Blake in her office.

She was even older than I remembered from when my sister had died. I guessed she didn't plan on retiring. She'd go straight from this office to her grave, and God help the poor soul who tried to make it otherwise.

"It's good to see you again, Emily." She said it without it seeming to click in her mind what she was saying. Seeing me again almost guaranteed I was going in some way off the beam.

It amazed me someone so highly trained in human behavior couldn't see her own. But I smiled politely and took a seat. The smile took more energy than I expected, and I was grateful to have a couch to collapse onto.

"I understand you're having a hard time dealing with what's happened to you."

I stared blankly at her. Was this the part where I was supposed to pour my soul out to her? Just because it was expected?

"Do you want to talk about it?" she asked, pulling a tape recorder from her desk drawer.

"I would prefer it if you didn't record our sessions."

I was uneasy about it for several reasons. Partly my semi-celebrity status. Recordings were more damning than notes. And also because it made it all too real.

She looked as if she might protest, but then her lips met in a firm line and she nodded, placing it back in the desk before retrieving a yellow legal pad.

"Very well then."

She arched a brow at me as if questioning whether I would now take issue with her making notes.

I had intended to sit on the couch, but I laid down on it instead, pulling my feet up with me. On the outside I'm sure this behavior indicated some willingness on my part to surrender to the therapy process, but it was really a way to hide. Lying down, I could look up at the ceiling and not meet her eyes.

"Shall we begin?" she asked.

"Actually, I just thought maybe you could give me something; write me a prescription. Valium, Zoloft, Prozac, anything." I wanted something to numb me out, make things blur around the edges a bit, but I didn't say that.

"Emily, now you know that's not how I operate."

Then I was going to have to find someone who did. With all the outcry at shrinks who doled out prescriptions like legal and politically-correct drug dealers, surely I could find someone to give me my fix of normal.

She sat patiently waiting, her pen poised, her attention rapt. I laid there for several minutes, the silence stretching between us. I kept waiting for her to say something. She kept waiting for me to say something. It was a battle of wills. I glanced occasionally at the clock on the wall as the minutes dragged on much more slowly than they ever had, even in the bad cell.

I wondered if I could use up my entire session like this. A complete hour of blissful silence. There was a time the prospect would have been deeply uncomfortable to me. I wouldn't have been able to resist the urge, the need, to fill the silent spaces with words.

Finally I did speak, but it wasn't because of discomfort with silence. I don't know what it was. It was the office, her patience, the comfortable couch, and the almost hypnotic lulling of the ticking of the wall clock. It was as if a trance had come over me, some sort of psychological possession that made me intent to spill, if not my secrets, then my feelings about them.

"I don't fit anymore," I began. "I don't know where to go from here. There is my life before, and my life now, and there's no bridge between the two. There is no way for me to go back to who I was."

"What about your life when you were where you were?" She avoided words like *captive* and *imprisoned.*

I stared up at the ceiling. I'm sure another five minutes passed before I spoke. "I can't tell you about that. It's private."

"What can you tell me about?"

I shrugged.

She decided to switch to a more direct question and answer approach, something easier and requiring less explanation on my part.

"How many people had you?"

"One."

"Male or female?"

"Male."

"You want to go back to him."

It wasn't a question. I bolted up from the couch and stared at her. Despite understandings of the victim/tormentor relationship, most people refused to accept someone wanting to go back after they were free.

"Yes," I said.

"Emily, you've got your masters in psychology. You know what this is. You know it's not real."

Was that true? It was one thing to pontificate about nameless strangers, it was another to experience it. It was difficult to imagine that in my position Dr. Blake would see things in the same way she saw them right now.

Of what use was it to struggle to keep everything the same? People changed. Did the catalyst matter? I shrugged again.

"Can you tell me anything of what happened while you were with him?"

I shook my head. No, I couldn't talk about that. It felt like betrayal. And I hated she knew that was why I couldn't talk about it. I could feel her pity from across the room.

Poor confused Emily.

"I'd really like some drugs," I said.

It was nearing the end of the session, and no progress had been made. For a brief moment, I imagined myself lying in a tub full of warm water while a peaceful buzz flowed over me, the bathwater going pink like Valentine's Day from my blood. Her voice cut off the fantasy.

"I'll tell you what. I'm going to give you some homework. I would like for you to keep a journal this next week of as much as you feel you can share, and we'll discuss it during next week's session. If you can do that for me, then we'll talk about prescribing something."

Blackmail.

It was the socially-approved equivalent of *blow me, and I'll get you some of the good stuff.* But I only nodded.

She was scribbling furiously on the yellow legal pad as I got up to leave. I had no idea what brilliant insights she felt she'd gleaned from my psyche in such a short period. I wasn't sure I wanted to know.

Since I had the car, I drove to the bookstore and picked out a journal. What the hell? I would go through my journal back in the Mercedes and copy the least revealing and private entries. I was sure enough emotion and trauma had gone into writing them.

I'd immediately rejected the notion of giving her the original journal. Besides being too personal, she might hand it over to the police as evidence. It was more violation than I could accept. I didn't need more strangers trying to peer into the most private parts of me.

By the time I got to the storage facility, the sun was going down. I sat in the Mercedes crying as I copied journal entries while listening to the music I'd missed having for weeks.

I'm not sure how much time passed sitting in the car. Although the storage facility wasn't on the main drag, I knew I took some measure of risk sitting there with the garage-style door open and the car running to play the music.

I copied several sections into the journal I'd just bought. It was heavily censored, but compared to today's session I was pouring my heart out. It would be enough to get me medicated, then I'd switch doctors.

I didn't need someone prying into my head, taking me apart bit by bit so they could put me back together again the way they felt I was supposed to be.

When I got home, I slipped the censored journal under the mattress of the bed in the guest room. Dinner was on the table, and my mother didn't say a word to me as she dipped food out onto my plate.

No, *Where have you been? Why didn't you call? I thought you'd driven into a lake or something.* She was gritting her teeth, but she was holding it in.

"Why the hell didn't you call? Your appointment was for an hour. You didn't think maybe I might need the car for something?"

Or not.

I didn't say anything. Instead, I picked up my plate and took it to the guest room and shut the door. I clicked on the TV with the remote and scooted back up on the bed leaning against the wicker headboard.

I knew I was behaving like a twelve-year-old, but I'd learned from experience it was better to steer clear of my mother when she was in this mode.

I pulled the journal out from under the bed again. It was light brown with Celtic knotwork. I traced a finger over the delicate design with one hand, as I absently shoveled chicken casserole into my mouth with the other. I'd filled about thirty pages of the book, surely enough for homework and drugs.

I Love Lucy was playing on low in the background. The canned laughter filtered over to me on the bed.

For a moment I thought about turning him in. What if? I was still angry with him for throwing me away. Shouldn't he be punished for that? Even if it seemed like he was being punished for something quite different? He'd know the real reason.

I tried to imagine the look on his face when the squad cars pulled into his driveway. Would he be remorseful? Ashamed? Shocked? Accepting? Would he adjust to imprisonment as well as I had?

I wondered again if he believed freeing me had been a cruelty or a kindness, if he thought he'd done something wrong in taking me. I wondered if he regretted letting me go, and if he ever thought of me or dreamed of me as I did him. Surely my obsession couldn't now be greater than his.

Would I be in trouble for lying and obstructing justice? Would someone lock me in a cell no matter how brief the time, thinking it was okay because I hadn't told the truth to the all-powerful police arm of the government?

Or could I play the fear card? *He terrorized me too much to speak. I was afraid he'd come for me again.* I didn't know.

But although the revenge fantasy was appealing for a moment, it quickly faded, replaced with the same feeling I always got when thinking of him as anything but omnipotent. Anxiety.

The next day was different. I don't know if it was seeing Dr. Blake or if the reality of my freedom had finally sunk in, but I started to get things together. I looked for an apartment, a small one. I had enough in the bank to see me through a year maybe while I tried to figure out what to do with the rest of my life.

I would adjust and be okay. I'd find my place in the world again, and this would just be something I'd experienced, but not something that had changed the core of who I was. I could be cured. I'd go through all the standard trauma responses, and then at the end of it I would be a *survivor.*

I could be unbrainwashed. It would require new conditioning, but it could be done. I could be free of him forever, mentally as well as physically.

It wasn't minor fame that gave me the money to take care of myself now, but extreme responsibility with my finances. I'd always been a saver instead of a spender. It was part of why this step scared me.

But I had to act. Otherwise, I was going to wither away and die in my parents' house in the creepy room with the white wicker furniture and the paper border wisteria dripping down from the edges of the ceiling.

I was too cowardly to kill myself, though I'd had fleeting fantasies. My master had thrown me out with finality, and my life with him was over. The only thing left to do was act.

To anyone observing this tragedy, I was a brave little soldier. Emily Vargas, the inspiration to kidnapped women everywhere. Such strength to so quickly begin putting the pieces of her life back together after all the horrors she must have suffered spending months at the hands of a madman.

I'd been invited already on a few talk shows to share my story, but I'd declined. No one was getting an exclusive. No one was getting the story period.

Everything seemed normal on the outside. But no one was there to hear me wake up crying in the middle of the night, reaching out for the comfort of a man's body that wasn't there. I dreamed only of him. Nothing else. There seemed to be nothing I could do to purge him from the darkest corners of my mind.

Thanksgiving came. Almost four weeks away from him and I couldn't even begin to not want him. I went to my parents' house for the obligatory turkey dinner. It was always a big deal. My cousins and uncles and aunts, my parents. My remaining set of grandparents on my dad's side. And of course friends, including Bobby White, the guy who'd grown up two houses down from me and had always had a crush.

Before being taken, I'd finally consented to one date with him. *Just to see*, as he'd said. He was seated at the main table directly across from me, staring at me over the large shiny basted turkey that looked like it should be in a food magazine.

I looked down at my plate. I couldn't stand to see the mixture of pity and self-absorbed disappointment that his one shot with me was probably gone for good.

My mom, as always, was the spokesperson for Thanksgiving. Granddad was the patriarch, but both he and Dad were men of few words, and mom had never had that problem. Like me. Or like I'd once been. I stared at my plate, tracing the filigree pattern around the edges with my finger, trying not to hear her as she said what she was thankful for, my safe return.

Various family members exclaimed their agreement, and I never felt so distant from them. Who were these people? I was a stranger here. We shared blood but not much else, and I wondered why we continued to get together every year like this. Like some bizarre mockery of the family unit.

Dinner went quickly and then there was pumpkin pie. I took my pie on a paper plate and went to sit on the couch in the living room. Several family members attempted polite conversation that skirted delicately around the facts of my absence. It was as if I'd been away at Summer Camp.

Four weeks before, every one of these people had been wearing black and attending my funeral, and now, here we were as if none of it had happened. The denial seemed to stretch out to all my family, to all I knew. Or thought I knew.

I sat with the paper plate propped on my knees as their voices turned into one big white noise machine. I felt the couch dip beside me but kept my focus on the pie. If I didn't acknowledge whoever it was, maybe they would go away.

Or at least just be fucking quiet.

"You've got more whipped cream than pie," Bobby said.

I glanced over to see him sitting beside me, his paper plate propped carefully on his lap mirroring mine, except for the modest amount of whipped cream, as if indulging in more would be a mortal sin.

"Yeah," I said and looked back at it.

I'd tried begging out of Thanksgiving dinner, telling my mother it was too much, too soon. It was partly true. It was too much, but I didn't think a timetable made a difference in the grand scheme of things. It would still be too much five years from now. I'd been irrevocably changed, and no one wanted to accept it, not even me.

They all wanted to believe with enough therapy and enough time, my world would be lovely again. I'd be their golden girl again, but despite my brief forays into fantasy land, I knew it wasn't true.

Mom had insisted I come. Everybody would feel bad if I wasn't there. And we wouldn't want that. I'd been avoiding them all for weeks. They missed me. Etc. etc. I'd caved because you always caved with my mother if you knew what was good for you. She wouldn't leave you alone to make a decision. She'd just harp until she got the answer she wanted. I regretted giving it now.

Most of the family was crowded in the other room around the new giant screen plasma television watching football. None of them were football fans, and most of them knew nothing about the game. They sat and watched football because it was what families did on Thanksgiving, or what they thought they were supposed to do.

We were all doing what we were supposed to do, and I wondered if even one of us was doing what he wanted to do. I glanced up to see Bobby staring at me intently. Well, one person was doing what they wanted to do.

Good for Bobby.

"Are you going to be okay?" he said.

"Yeah," I lied.

Part of me hated him right then. Either he was too clueless to understand the nature of my captivity made it completely inappropriate for him to bring it up, or worse, he was hoping to score points as the knight in shining armor who comforted me. I couldn't deal with being a pawn in his fantasy right then.

He reached out and put his hand over mine. I jerked away and scooted to the far end of the couch. I couldn't stand for anyone to touch me. Or at least I couldn't stand for anyone but one person to touch me.

"Sorry," he mumbled. "Jeez Emmie, that fucking bastard fucked you up good, didn't he?"

"Don't say that!" I was shocked by the vehemence of my voice.

"Aw, hell. You know I didn't mean anything against you. I just wish I could get him alone in a room, you know?"

I couldn't meet his eyes because I knew he'd see the anger boiling just beneath the surface. There was a chance he'd think the anger was directed at my captor. But there was a chance, however small, that he wouldn't.

"Emmie?"

"Yeah," I said, acknowledging his empty threat toward my master.

I don't know why I was angry. Bobby wouldn't have a shot in a room alone with him. I knew I hadn't just built my captor up in my mind as physically stronger than he was because of how helpless he'd made me.

I'd seen his well-muscled body many times, felt his weight on me, the strength of his grip. I knew. He'd rip Bobby to pieces, and I couldn't decide whether that idea upset me or not. It upset me a lot less than the idea of Bobby hurting *him.*

"Alright, well, um . . . I need to really get going. But if you ever need somebody to talk to, you know where I am, yeah?" He was edging toward the door.

"Yeah."

He looked at me another long moment before turning and walking off with his empty paper plate. His shoulders slumped. I had been right. He'd had a picture in his head about how his love would heal me or some other similar romantic bullshit. He'd be my rescuer. But what if I no longer wanted to be rescued?

One by one family members and friends trickled into the room to have a word with me, to tell me how much they'd missed me, how glad they were I was safe. If I needed anything . . . By the time they'd all paraded through, I was crying and couldn't stop. I waited until they left, and then I got in my car and went home.

My mother had seen me upset and seemed to regret persuading me to come. I'm not sure if it was because some perfect, mythic Thanksgiving was ruined or she really felt bad. We never spoke of it.

That week I put in resumes at several places. My publisher called, but I had no intention to continue writing, at least not self-help books. "Maybe a memoir," they said. I said, "Maybe," but didn't mean it. I was done. It was time to move on to something else.

The day of my next appointment with Dr. Blake, I sat in my apartment looking at all my stuff. The bookshelves with my books lining them, a couple bags of fan mail that had piled up while I'd been away. This was freedom. This was what I wanted, what I'd yearned for, for months. Or at least until I knew it wasn't possible and I'd given up the hope.

I didn't think I could ever do public speaking again. I wasn't sure if I could write, at least not that sort of book anymore, the kind that changed people's lives for the better and made them go after their goals and believe in themselves. All of it now seemed like pat phrases and cheap pop psychology. How had I taken my knowledge and boiled it down to such black-and-white simplicity?

Maybe I would go into research like I'd originally planned. Don a lab coat and stay out of the spotlight. As I rode the elevator up to the fifth floor for my session, I held out the fragile hope everything hadn't ended for me.

"You look a bit better this week. I take it the journaling was helpful? Cathartic maybe?"

I nodded, a nonverbal lie. I looked better because I was employing the *fake it til you make it* technique, acting as if I were fine in the vain hope it would make it so.

I handed her the journal and stretched out on the couch while she flipped through it.

"This is more than I expected. I'm very pleased." She said it as if I were a dog eager for a biscuit.

I didn't care one way or the other about her approval, but I smiled anyway. It was easier to just go along.

If I went along and cooperated, she'd write me a prescription at the end of the session, and hopefully a combination of drugs and life itself would make me free of him. Happy.

I waited while she read and felt suddenly self-conscious. Though I hadn't revealed everything, or even the most graphic things that had happened during my enslavement, it was enough. It was far more intimate a portrait of those days than I would share with anyone who wasn't offering drugs to numb it all down to a pleasant fuzziness.

Finally, she closed the journal and looked up. "Thank you for sharing this with me. Would you like to tell me why it's all written in third person, though?"

I don't know why I said it, I just blurted the first thing that came into my head. "It's not about me. It's just a story."

I was less shocked at having said it, and more shocked that it was true.

I had dissociated. Every sexual encounter I'd written as if it had happened to someone else.

I closed my eyes and went back, remembering, seeing his eyes, his hands on my body, not someone else's. I expected to feel revulsion, fear, panic, disgust, but what I felt instead was much more disturbing. I felt the heat surge between my legs, the wetness of my panties, and full-on arousal.

I was barely there through the rest of the session, on autopilot, responding as the doctor expected, until the session was over and it was time to write a prescription. She scribbled something on the prescription pad and handed me the journal, telling me to keep up the good work and she'd see me next week.

I stopped off at the bathroom on the way out, ashamed of my physical reaction in the doctor's office and what I was about to do, but I needed release. I locked the door behind me and unzipped my pants, letting them fall in a whisper to the floor. I leaned forward against the door, one hand pressed against the cold metal, anchoring me as I brought myself to orgasm with the other.

His face was in my mind as I came, stifling a moan. I pulled my pants back up, my fingers trembling as I buttoned them. I washed my hands in the sink. The soap smelled like the soap from my elementary school. I didn't look at my face in the mirror. I didn't want to see my eyes.

After getting my prescription filled, I wandered through the city. I left my car in the parking garage and took a cab. Before I knew where I'd asked the driver to take me, I was sitting in front of the Atlanta Zoo.

I paid the fare and shoved the prescription bottle into my bag. I'd expressed, not primarily depression, but anxiety in Dr. Blake's office, a skittish jumpiness around loud noises, too many people, social situations.

And the truth was, I'd so often stayed in the house watching television because going out made me nervous. I'd managed to have a burst of courage for about a week to get out of my parents' house, but it was coming quickly to an end.

And so I had a bottle containing a two-week supply of Xanax. Not quite Valium, but who's complaining? My hand gripped the bottle nestled in my purse for comfort, and I went to the zoo.

I stopped off at one of the little cafeterias and had lunch, fattening greasy fried food. Chicken, potato salad, baked beans. Staples of the south. Comfort food. I wandered, observing the animals in their cages.

I hadn't been to the zoo as an adult. It had always bothered me watching animals in cages like a creepy voyeur while acting like it was good clean fun. But I could identify with their plight now, and I didn't feel nearly as bad for them as I would have at one time.

None of them seemed distressed. I couldn't quite believe they didn't know what was going on, but at the same time, they seemed okay with it. Safe. Secure. Knowing they were taken care of, that they didn't have to face the big bad world and participate in the cruel dance for survival as others of their kind did.

Some of them were lying around; some of them were playing and doing goofy antics for the crowds that had gathered, especially the bears and monkeys. They always tended to perform.

A large group of children on a school field trip rushed to the monkey cage near where I stood looking on. I jumped and moved out of the way, unable to deal with the sudden noise and flutter of activity. Each of the children had a brightly-colored balloon tied around his or her wrist. A woman about my age shouted to quiet them.

"Blue balloons need to go with Miss Patti to *The Wild Planet Cafe* for lunch. Red and yellow balloons stay where you are."

More children ran up then with green balloons and a haggard Miss Patti for the shift change. I slipped into a man-made cave nearby that was air-conditioned and had videos. My pulse raced as my anxiety crept higher. They were only children, but it felt like a close brush with death.

I focused on one of the screens to distract myself, my hand skimming over the surface to find a knob to turn up the volume. The video showed a crowd of angry PETA members protesting the cruelty of keeping animals in cages at the zoo. Painted signs and morally outraged faces filled the screen.

A voice-over began to play. "In our modern age, some are concerned about the practice of keeping animals caged. Although this is a valid concern, unfortunately once an animal has lived in captivity for so long, it's more cruel to release them back into the wild. They no longer have the survival skills. This is more true for those born into captivity, but is also true for adult animals who haven't always been with us."

I glanced back over at the monkey cages, and one of the chimpanzees showed his teeth to me. It looked like a smile, and I wasn't sure if I was trying to give him human characteristics or if it really was an expression of happiness. Then he screeched a couple of times and went off to play with the others.

I waited for the children to move on to the next exhibit, and when there was a clear path I went to a less crowded area. I stood on a bridge with dozens of dispensers of duck food you could get at a quarter a pop. I gripped the railing and gazed into the dark water, taking slow, measured breaths.

Was this how it would always be? Such anxiety and agitation out in the open air? Would I add agoraphobia to the ever-growing list? I dug through my purse for the pill bottle. My body shook as I deposited a pill into my hand. I was about to pop it into my mouth when I stopped and stared at it.

Then for no reason I can explain, I dropped the little oval lie into the lake. A duck went for it but then swam away. My hand tilted slowly until the rest of the lies tumbled out and then dropped like tiny pebbles into the water. A crowd of ducks swam over, pecking at the pills, then left them swirling, squawking and upset they'd been tricked. I knew the feeling.

I dug in my pocket for a quarter and cranked the machine where the duck food was. The ducks deserved to have what they wanted and so did I. It no longer mattered to me what anyone else expected. Like my master, I had become separated from society.

I wasn't a part anymore, and the old rules no longer applied. They only applied if I wanted to be a part, and I found that I didn't. Of what use would a life based on a past reality be? I wasn't the same woman anymore, and I no longer wanted to be free.

I regretted now digging up the coffin the month before. Emily Vargas should have stayed buried. I sprinkled the duck food into the water and went to get the Mercedes.

Twelve

I knew now why I'd written reverse directions. I'd never believed I would get lost. I'd always known I was going back. I just wanted a final taste of the freedom on the other side, like a bride intent on one last hoorah before her wedding day.

I wrote and mailed a letter to my parents knowing they'd never understand, but wishing somehow they could.

I felt a sense of smugness knowing the feds would be picking apart Nebraska looking for me, if they even made the attempt. Hopefully, crazy-induced or not, my letter would be seen as an insistence that they just let me be. It had been wrong to go back and give them false hope.

In my defense, I hadn't done it on purpose. I'd believed for small moments at a time that there *was* hope. But the only thing I longed for was to be back in his arms again, and I knew that would never change.

Maybe the doctor could cure me. I could be doped up on drugs and reconditioned in an office where I was told over and over again it wasn't my fault. That was the thing of it though, while I'd been stupid in leaving my drink unattended, I'd never believed I deserved it. I knew being captured wasn't my fault.

I hadn't thought I was bad. It could have been because he didn't have words at his disposal to break me down in that way. Maybe if he'd had speech and told me over and over it was my fault, I would have believed it. But that hadn't happened. I just craved that silent strength and power. I couldn't stop myself.

I didn't care how I'd gotten to this desire, only that I was here. He was the one thing in my life that made any kind of sense, and I didn't know his name. I knew even if he took me back, I would probably never know his name. Only *Master.*

I pulled up to the house and turned off the ignition. I was wearing clothes he'd given me, the journal and CD's clutched tightly in my hands. I knocked on the door and waited.

Was he even home? I'd persisted in the odd belief that he sat around all the time watching me on the video monitors, as if in doing so he was equally enslaved to me.

It was a beautiful day, one of those rare unseasonably warm days the south sometimes gets in December.

The sun was shining, the birds chirping, a light warm breeze blowing, and yet it felt stifling. Too open. Unsafe. Finally, the door opened.

Somehow I'd imagined he'd fall apart without me. He'd regret releasing me and be glad to have me back. But there was nothing disheveled or unkempt about his appearance. No hair out of place, and he was well-dressed. As always.

He regarded me with that arrogant coldness that somehow hadn't seemed so cold when I'd been on the other side of that door. And suddenly I wasn't so sure I had a place here anymore.

"Master, please . . . "

He shut the door and locked it. I banged on the door for at least twenty minutes but nothing came of it. I slid to the ground on the massive porch and leaned against the heavy dark-stained wood. Had he really gotten bored with me?

He was just done? It was over because he said it was? I knew I should have gotten back in the car and gone home. I could intercept the letter when it arrived at my parents' house and burn it. No one ever had to know any of this. I could go back to my therapy appointments and resume their plans for me. To get better. To recover. To survive.

I was angry he would turn me away like this. I should turn him in if he wouldn't take me back, but I still couldn't do it.

My knuckles were bleeding. The last time they'd bled, I'd been begging to be set free. I let out a hysterical peal of laughter. A few minutes passed, and the door opened a few inches. Before I could get up, it was shut and locked again. I looked down. A water bottle, soft washcloth, ointment, and bandages for my hands.

Now I knew the game. I could see no reason he would help me if he really had lost interest. He'd never been that cruel. As with everything, the choice was up to me.

However sick, twisted, or perverse it was, this was the most free choice I'd ever been given. I'd been completely safe, not in any way dependent upon him, and yet, here I was a month later, begging on his door-step like some stray to be taken in.

A month out in the world and all I had to show for it was a lot of mindless television and a few visits to the shrink's office. I carefully poured half the bottle of water onto the cloth. I gritted my teeth as I cleaned the torn skin on my knuckles. Then came the soothing aloe gel and the bandages. I drank the rest of the water and waited.

I reread my journal, the original. The other one, the sanitized copy, was still in the car. Here it was, every single thing he'd done to me and every single thing I'd submitted to so he wouldn't put me back in the bad cell. Emotions, feelings, degrading sexual acts.

I knew how I was supposed to react, but I couldn't call forth those feelings. Reading each scene described in vivid detail like erotica, I could feel the wetness pooling between my legs.

A couple of hours passed. I thought about knocking again, but my hands hurt too much. Besides, I had no doubt he knew I was out here still. If I kept banging, he might keep me locked out longer.

I carried on with the persistent belief that he'd open the door and let me back in, that this was the final test. I just had to prove my worthiness.

Finally the door opened, and he slipped a bowl of chicken noodle soup, crackers, and another bottled water outside before closing the door and locking me out again. I couldn't stop the smile that spread over my face. God, I'd completely lost my mind. I crumbled the crackers into the soup and ate. Everything was turning around on me. The soup was comforting again because it meant hope. He was engaging with me.

That night clouds rolled in, and it started to rain. Thunder rumbled, and lightning flashed across the sky. The winds picked up and started to blow rainwater onto the porch.

The night and the rain brought a dip in temperature; it wasn't quite cold, but it wasn't comfortable anymore. I shivered and huddled into the corner of the porch, farthest from the path of the blowing rain.

I stared longingly at the Mercedes sitting a few feet away, unlocked. I could get inside and turn on the heater and lie curled on the back seat until the gas tank ran dry. But I didn't want to be farther away from him, in case he let me in.

Around midnight the door opened again, and pillows and heavy blankets were tossed out.

I moved back to the corner of the porch and huddled in the blankets until I fell asleep. When morning came, there was a new chill on the air, weather much more befitting of December. I snuggled deeper into the wool fabric, wondering if he'd let me freeze to death on his porch.

Soon, strong arms scooped me up and carried me into the house. He sat me down on the couch in the room we'd been in that last day, and left. He returned several minutes later with fresh clothes from the closet of the good cell.

I held them uncertainly.

He crossed his arms over his chest and raised a brow at me. I hesitated for just a moment. Being free for weeks had caused bits of my modesty to come back, but my desire to stay with him, whatever the cost, overcame that false wall I'd re-erected around myself.

I peeled the old, still slightly damp, clothing from my body. I was aware of the consuming way he stared at me, as if assessing whether I was worth keeping, as if I were a slave up at auction. If he let me stay, it might be a long-term investment.

I was oddly proud of myself for maintaining the shaving and how it displayed my obedience to him even from a distance. I put the other clothes on and then sat on the couch, looking up at him expectantly.

Finally, he signed. *Why are you here? I told you to go. I released you.*

"I don't want to be released. I want to stay."

It's wrong to keep you here.

"It's more wrong to set me free! Don't you see what you've done to me?"

He shook his head and crossed the room to take my arm. His grip was punishing, much more rough than he normally handled me, unless we were in the dungeon and he was whipping me for his sexual gratification.

He led me to the door, and I knew he was throwing me out for good. If he managed to get me outside, that was it. I knew he'd let me die on the porch from exposure or starvation before he'd ever open the door to me again.

I tried to pull away from him, tears streaming down my cheeks. "Master, please don't do this."

He dragged me down the hallway, ignoring my pleas. Finally, I got angry. Rage like I'd felt at the cemetery as I'd dug down through six feet of earth as if I could bring back something that was long gone.

"NO!" I jerked free of him. It wasn't that I was stronger or had suddenly developed superpowers. It was that the vehemence and determination had surprised him enough to cause him to loosen his grip.

I backed further into the house, grabbing a candlestick that was sitting on a table in the entryway. An antique candlestick that probably cost more than I'd made in a month back when I'd been *Emily Vargas, self-help guru.*

He smiled at me, his eyes alight with genuine amusement. We both knew I couldn't overpower him, even with a weapon. He could easily disarm me and throw me outside. Still, he stood back, his arms crossed again over his chest, waiting to see what I'd do. I'd just become interesting to him again.

Good for me.

"Just fucking listen to me!" My voice was stronger than it had ever been with him. I had nothing left to lose.

I wasn't afraid of him anymore. I was only afraid of being without him.

I kept the candlestick raised. "Don't you see how fucked up this is? You think it's wrong to keep me? Well you should have thought about that shit before you took me! I'm your responsibility now. You created me. You made me this way. This is your fucking mess. If you suddenly care about morality, then don't make me go. Let me stay. I'll be your slave. I'll be your whore. I'll never fight you. I won't disobey. Whatever you want, just don't make me go back. Please. I can't live in that world anymore. You know it's true. I just want to be yours."

Are you finished?

I nodded, deflated. He left me standing in the entryway, and when he returned he held the highest object of fear. A knife. He advanced, but I didn't back away.

He gripped me by the throat and held me against the wall, the knife poised to strike. The cool blade was pressed underneath my chin. His eyes were hard and unrelenting.

"I don't care. Do it. Kill me or keep me, but don't you fucking dare throw me away again." Then I added, "Please."

I didn't flinch or look away from his eyes. Finally, he flung the knife away and kissed me. His hands gripped my wrists tightly as he held them against the wall. His tongue delved deeper into my mouth, and I opened to him and submitted everything.

Then he stepped back from me and unzipped his pants before pushing me to my knees in front of him. I took his cock into my mouth without hesitation, sucking him until he came, and I swallowed.

Adrenaline buzzed through me like a living thing. I stayed on my knees at his feet looking up at him, waiting for his next order.

You're going to be punished.

"For what?" For leaving him when he'd forced me to? For staying away so long? For coming back and making him face himself? The monster he was and the pitiable creature he'd turned me into.

For the disrespectful way you just spoke to me. If you stay, the rules aren't changing.

I nodded, a hard lump forming in my throat. "Three weeks?" I asked. My voice was so small again.

It was almost as long as I'd been free. Three weeks was an unthinkable amount of time to spend in the bad cell.

You could leave.

I shook my head. It was only three weeks out of my entire life. I could make it.

"Do you still want me?"

If I didn't, you wouldn't have made it through the door.

I took his outstretched hand and followed him.

When we reached the cell, something passed between us. Perhaps it was the close bond we'd formed over the months coming back in full force, but it was like a telepathic link between us, and as I looked into his eyes, I could see the truth.

He'd never been sorry for taking me. He still wasn't sorry. Not for one thing he'd done. It had been for his own sadistic pleasure that he'd made me make the choice.

Just as he'd forced me to choose to let him rape me or leave me in the cell forever. Just like he'd forced me to accept the riding crop, the whip, the cane, and everything else he'd ever introduced.

I'd just turned my back on any chance at freedom because he was never letting me go now. He smiled when he saw the realization on my face, and he turned to leave, the door sealing shut with deafening finality.

I had been free and I'd walked right back into my cage. I'd begged and fought to be let in, and the entire time I'd been playing his game exactly the way he wanted it played. I hadn't convinced him to keep me. He'd always intended on me coming back to him. Just one more damning choice.

What the hell had I done? Was I truly this far gone? No textbook in existence could have prepared me for what I'd experienced.

I sat in the empty cell trying to think if the truth of it made a difference. Would I have come back if I'd been sure this was what he was doing?

The answer remained the same. Yes. No matter how desperately I wanted to, I couldn't bring myself to hate him.

But it wasn't love either. What we shared was deeper than love. It was a mad and unyielding obsession, and it was mutual. And the flames from it would likely kill one of us some day. Probably me. I couldn't bring myself to care. I'd rather have this intensity with him than a hundred years of mediocrity with another.

I moved to my corner and waited. Minutes later the door opened as I knew it would, as if I'd called out to him with my mind to tell him I was sitting where I was supposed to be. But I knew the truth. His eyes had probably been glued to the video monitors from the moment he'd locked me back in here. He brought in my bathing supplies and fresh clothes.

"I'm on my period."

I thought he might give me something, instead of making me go around naked, but he smiled and took the vile plain clothing away.

There was a time I would have questioned his smile, but our minds had worked to move in sync, thinking each other's thoughts before the other had them. It was fitting that I should be reduced to this animalistic state once again. I'd been away too long in freedom, the ability to come and go as I pleased, to have privacy, to have modesty.

Now it was being stripped away from me all at once. But I don't think he fully understood. He may have believed he knew, but he couldn't possibly know what he'd unleashed within me. I was only free with him. He was the first person who'd seen me in every state imaginable and still wanted me. I'd never been so bare with anyone else.

I bathed and left my clothing by the door and went to sleep in my corner. It was still daylight I knew, early in the day in fact, but I needed a nap.

As I drifted off, I tried not to think about how time would all bleed together, the unsettling lack of knowledge about what day it was or what time it was, not knowing if the sun was in the sky or if it was the dead of night.

I dreamed of the good cell and the scented candles, the studio and old ballet records, the incense and rows upon rows of books. I dreamed of his face, his hands on my skin, his cock buried deep inside me while my unresisting body accepted each inch of him.

When my period was over, he brought me fresh clothes again. I didn't try to fight or tempt him. I put them on and waited out my time. I didn't want to make it four weeks.

Slowly the days were marked off. The chicken noodle soup came three times a day until I couldn't stand the sight of it, until once again it was the vile punishment it had been intended as.

Finally, the three weeks were up, and he stepped into my cell. My heart thrummed with anticipation. I had sworn to myself I'd never give him any reason to lock me in the cell for three weeks, and I had broken that vow. Now I swore I would never be in the cell for four. I would never disobey or disrespect him again.

Even as I thought it, I knew it wasn't true. I wondered how long it would be before I did something to send me back. I wondered if one day I'd be in the cell so long I'd lose my mind or forget what his face looked like. And I found that the second would be the worse punishment. I could handle being crazy if I could still look at him.

He held the blindfold out, and I stepped forward, allowing him to cover my eyes with the soft black fabric. I wondered if he'd ever let me roam the house freely, if it was something I could eventually earn. I would work up the nerve to ask him that someday, but not today.

Today, I allowed him to lead me out of the cell. My heart rate quickened as I heard the key code being punched in, first at the bad cell, and then at the door he'd brought me to. When he removed the blindfold, I knew this was where I'd find myself today.

The dungeon.

He approached me, but then backed away. Normally he'd done what he wanted, no communication but touch passing between us. He held my gaze, and then he signed.

Strip, slowly.

I'd been his willing toy for so many months, allowing him to play with me however he saw fit. I hadn't seen myself as an active participant, not until now, when language finally broached our world together.

My fingers shook as I reached for the buttons of my top and undid them, slowly swaying to music I heard only in my head. Music he'd given me that I'd never heard until him. I stood naked, watching, waiting for his next command.

Do you want to be whipped?

The throbbing between my legs intensified as if he'd pushed a button. "Yes, Master."

I looked down, suddenly shy and unsure. The fucked-up thing was that I did want him to whip me. I wanted him to do with me whatever would please him.

In two quick strides, he was in front of me. He gripped my chin painfully and forced me to meet his eyes. They were so stormy I couldn't read the emotion in them. I felt for once the communication that had always flowed between us in silence had been shut down, broken through a more lazy form of speech.

You know I can't talk to you if you don't look at me.

"I'm sorry. It's just so . . . strange. I . . . I'm sorry. It won't happen again."

He must have seen the fear in my eyes, that I was going back to be punished again for such a small offense.

I'm not putting you back in the cell, as long as you try to obey. You know that. I know you didn't do it on purpose. It is *strange.*

I smiled and he smiled back. It was the smile that didn't scare me, the one that made me feel inexplicably safe despite everything. He led me to the velvet bed and positioned me on my knees, locking the chains around my ankles. My stomach tightened as he scanned the row of whips and floggers before settling on one.

He was behind me now and everything felt normal again without words in the way. The whip cracked across my back, the pain searing deeper than I remembered, but it felt like something, and it was immeasurably better than the nothingness I'd felt when I was free and when I'd been in the bad cell.

He stopped when he drew blood, then his cock was inside me, pounding into me so hard I could barely catch my breath. I felt my muscles contract around him, and then wave after wave of mindless pleasure crested over me as I let the tears flow freely down my face.

His hands skimmed across my flesh, cupping my breasts, stroking my back where the blood was slowly pooling. His touch was like heroin in my veins, and I was a grateful addict.

EPILOGUE

Doctor Blake sat in her office with the worn and well-read letter clutched tightly in her aging hand. Donna Vargas sat across from her, blissfully calm in a drug-induced haze. The letter had arrived that morning. Mrs. Vargas had used up her old prescription and was there for more.

If not for the strong effects of the still-potent drugs, Mrs. Vargas would no doubt have blamed Doctor Blake, and Doctor Blake would have felt it well-deserved. She'd known the state the daughter, Emily, had been in, how precarious it was.

She stared at the words scrawled on the paper, not really seeing them. The script in Emily's handwriting was obviously rushed, written in those last moments before she became just another statistic of one sort or another.

Like many doctors, she blamed herself. Knowing what she'd known, why hadn't she just broken her own damned rule and given the poor girl drugs the first week when she'd asked for them? Anything that would make her stable enough not to do this. If only she'd had more time with her; they'd barely begun her therapy.

She read the letter again. It was probably the fifth time she'd read it, but she knew even if she'd read it a hundred times, Mrs. Vargas would have read it more:

I know this letter will come as a shock, but please try to understand. I should have stayed buried. The moment I saw my name on the tombstone, I should have understood it was true.

I'm dead to you, and you were right to bury me. At first I was angry about it, but now I understand. I understand the need to erase me, and that's okay.

My only regret is that I came home. I don't think there is any way I can explain this to make it easier on you, but I'll try. You see, I've never been free. Not one day of my life. I've always given in to the wants and needs of those around me. My confidence has always been a social mask and my success as a motivational speaker was because my mask was just so damn convincing. At times, even to me.

But I've never followed my own will. What I wanted. It was always what you guys wanted. Or what society wanted. Or what college wanted. Or what anyone else who wasn't me and came into my life wanted. I had almost fallen for it again. I almost did what you all wanted.

I almost took my pills like a good little girl, had my cathartic trauma moment, and put the pieces of my world back together so everyone could say how brave and good I was. Almost. But I couldn't.

As I write this letter I can't decide whether I'm acting from strength or weakness, but I know that I'm acting for the first time from my own will. Yes, I know that's hard to accept. It wouldn't be my will if that monster hadn't taken me like he had, right?

You likely believe he's bent and twisted me to his liking, and now I can't get out of that mold. Perhaps. But I've been free for a month, and it sure as fuck doesn't feel like freedom, just a larger cage.

I don't see how pretending I'm free solves anything. I didn't want to leave him. I know. Stockholm Syndrome. Blah blah blah. I know. I know it's true, but I wasn't prepared for what it would mean for me. You see, I don't feel crazy. So I wonder who came up with these arbitrary labels. Who gets to decide?

Am I to be sane and miserable in a world of somebody else's creation or am I to be crazy, and in my own strange way, free?

He made me leave him. I cried and begged not to go, but ultimately I went because it was what he wanted. But this is the one order from him I just can't obey.

I suppose I could have done what I plan to do now, stayed and waited however long it took until he accepted me back. Until whatever guilt complex he may have developed, abated. Or until I passed whatever test he was giving.

But I was weak and came home to say my goodbyes. I know that probably didn't feel like goodbye. I was in denial for awhile that it was. And I'm sure that seeing the ghost of your daughter one more time wasn't as satisfying as anyone thought it might have been. But that's all that's left. A ghost of your daughter.

Even if you somehow miraculously found me, that hollowed-out empty shell would be all that would be left. I can't be that girl anymore. Still, I don't want you to worry, and at the same time I know it's ridiculous to expect you not to.

As for the man who has me, he's never put me in any physical harm. He's never done anything in all the months I've been with him that made me feel like my life was about to end or that I'd need hospitalization. It's never been like that between us.

I know it's impossible to comprehend or believe, but I feel safe with him. By the end of the second month, I think I was happy. I understand it's not love, and that's the part of me that thinks maybe I'm not crazy, if I can know that much.

But I know I need him. And I hope he needs me. What we have is fucked up and twisted, but it serves a need. I know I've always been wired differently. He only brought to the surface what was already there.

I'm not saying I'm glad it happened the way it did or that I believe it's somehow morally okay. But he's not cruel as you might imagine, and he's never lost control with me in all the time he's had me.

I'm sorry I couldn't play the role you needed me to play. I'm sorry I couldn't go to therapy and have the approved victim response and recover. I know you'll never be able to understand me making this choice. I know you'll all believe it was a sick mind that led me to it, that no person in their right mind would do what I've done. Maybe that's the truth of it.

Or maybe I'm just stronger than you.

CPSIA information can be obtained at www.ICGtesting.com
Printed in the USA
BVOW08*0300060815

411921BV00002B/17/P